ADDISON MOORE

Pumpkin Pie Parting

Murder in the Mix Mystery #15

Edited by Paige Maroney Smith
Cover by Lou Harper, Cover Affairs
Published by Hollis Thatcher Press, LTD.

Books by Addison Moore

Cozy Mystery

Cutie Pies and Deadly Lies (Murder in the Mix 1)
Bobbing for Bodies (Murder in the Mix 2)
Pumpkin Spice Sacrifice (Murder in the Mix 3)
Gingerbread and Deadly Dread (Murder in the Mix 4)
Seven-Layer Slayer (Murder in the Mix 5)
Red Velvet Vengeance (Murder in the Mix 6)
Bloodbaths and Banana Cake (Murder in the Mix 7)
New York Cheesecake Chaos (Murder in the Mix 8)
Lethal Lemon Bars (Murder in the Mix 9)
Macaron Massacre (Murder in the Mix 10)
Wedding Cake Carnage (Murder in the Mix 11)
Donut Disaster (Murder in the Mix 12)
Toxic Apple Turnovers (Murder in the Mix 13)
Killer Cupcakes (Murder in the Mix 14)
Pumpkin Pie Parting (Murder in the Mix 15)
Yule Log Eulogy (Murder in the Mix 16)

1

I see dead people. Mostly I see dead pets, but on the rare occasion I do see a dearly departed of the human variety. However, at the moment, I'm looking at a rather dead husband—namely mine.

"Noah!" I leap over him and offer a firm embrace.

We're standing outside of the Evergreen Manor, right in front of my refrigerated van where I'm about to extricate enough pumpkin pies to feed all of Vermont. It's the night of the Friendsgiving charity event at the Evergreen Manor, where proceeds go to helping families in need have all the supplies they'll need to have a Thanksgiving of their own. The parking lot is heavily scented by the pines in the nearby woods, and the icy air knifing through my dress certainly promises an early snowfall this year.

I pull back and examine his ghostly frame. He's every bit himself except for the fact he's glowing a faint shade of blue and I can see the forest behind him right through his body. But those loving—glowing in the literal sense—green eyes, those deep-welled dimples, the dark hair, the bodybuilder frame, he's every bit the same.

"How's it going, Lottie?" He lands a simple kiss to my lips and it feels strangely solid. I'm forever marveling at the fact that the ghosts that visit me have the capability to feel as solid as they want. And right about now Noah wants.

My chest bucks with emotion. "Better now that you're here. What's happening, Noah? Why *are* you here? Is someone that loved you about to bite the big one? Oh goodness, it's not me, is it?"

A laugh rumbles through his chest. "I promise, it's nothing like that. And for once, I am damn glad you are supersensual."

Noah is right about the supersensual thing—further classified as transmundane. I didn't always know what this strange gift was called, up until my grandmother Nell filled me in on it last Christmas. It turns out, she was supersensual, too, but she's long since passed.

The only people who know my secret are Noah and Everett, and, of course, my birth mother Carlotta who shares my eerie talent. I just met Carlotta last January. We're still trying to key in our relationship, but the fact we can see the dead has been a rather bonding experience to say the least.

"I'm glad I'm supersensual, too," I say, swooning at this gorgeous glowing version of the man I married. Okay, so Noah and I were accidentally married while working on an active homicide investigation. You see, we dated a year ago, and then I found out he conveniently forgot to mention he was still technically married to the woman I thought was his ex-wife, so I broke up with him until he could figure that mess out. And, in the meantime, I got hot and heavy with his former stepbrother, Judge Essex Everett Baxter. That sort of complicated things to no end.

Noah's father had married Everett's mother for a brief time, just long enough to swindle her out of part of her fortune. And while they were all living under the same ritzy roof out in Fallbrook, Noah saw it fit to steal Everett's girlfriend from under him, an up-and-coming socialite by the name of Cormack Featherby. They were all in high school at the time, and let's just say when they're together they can still act that way, too.

I pull back and marvel at the ghost of this beautiful man who stole my heart.

"Noah, you know the rules. I see a ghost and something bad happens to someone who had an affinity for the poltergeist. Sure, usually it's a cute fuzzy little animal coming back from the other side of the rainbow bridge, but it's been a person plenty of times before. And I haven't seen you since you nearly died." I swat him on the arm and my hand glides right through him. "How dare you stay away from me."

He's right back to chuckling. "I'm sorry, Lot. I haven't had too much control over where I land. I've been locked in that body of mine, trying my best to wake up."

I swallow hard. About a week ago, Noah and his psychotic ex-girlfriend Cormack Featherby were in a horrific car accident.

It was Halloween night and Cormack's father just gifted her a brand new steel gray Corvette, and she thought she'd take Noah for a quick spin. But as it turns out, Cormack missed a turn as she was speeding down a twisted road and smacked into an old oak tree going eighty miles an hour.

Cormack came out of it unscathed, but Noah is still in the hospital hanging on by the skin of his teeth—and the fact that his ghost is visiting me doesn't bode well for the situation.

Cormack has been pretty torn up about it. She's held vigil at the hospital almost as much as I have. Cormack Featherby was under the ripe delusion that Noah was her boyfriend when, in fact, Cormack has been nothing more than a proficient stalker of his.

"You're on life support, Noah. They put you in a medically induced coma hoping you'll heal quicker that way, but they've since tried taking you out if it..." I stop shy of telling him that his brain activity isn't looking all so great. I don't think I can bring myself to say the words. My chest bucks as I fight an onslaught of tears.

"I know." He nods and bites down on his lower lip as if trying to stave off his own emotions. "I hope you don't mind if I hang out tonight." He hitches his head toward the Evergreen Manor.

"Are you kidding? Noah, I never want you to leave."

"Is that Noah?" a deep voice calls out from behind, and I turn in time to see Everett making his way over in a dark, crisp suit. Everett is tall with broad shoulders, black hair, and cerulean blue eyes that make every female in a ten-mile radius sit up and pay attention. He's slow to smile and serious as one can get without turning to stone. He also happens to be painfully handsome, as is Noah.

"Yes! He's here!" I say, waving him over, and Everett quickly takes up my hand. A while back Everett and I discovered that others can hear the dead if they hold my hand. I don't know why, but I seem to act as a sort of a conduit.

"Noah"—Everett's chest expands the size of a door—"I love you, man. I'm sorry we haven't always gotten along, but you need to come back to us. Life isn't the same without you."

Noah's smile broadens. "It was almost worth crossing to the other side just to hear you say those words. I appreciate it. I suppose you're taking good care of Lottie." Noah's expression smooths out on a dime, but sadly he looks almost resigned to his current disembodied state.

"I am." Everett wraps an arm around my shoulders. "And not in the way you think. Lemon and I are still hoping the best for you."

He grunts, "Stranger things have happened."

"*Lottie?*" a female voice calls from the entry to the kitchen of the Evergreen Manor. I recognize that voice as my newly revealed cousin, Naomi Sawyer.

"I'd better get going," I say. "But you're coming with me, Noah. There's no way I'm letting you out of my sight."

"Actually"—Everett ticks his head to the side as he looks to Noah—"you should probably get back in that body of yours and try like hell to impress the doctors."

I suck in a quick breath. "That's true, Noah. If you're here, that can't mean good things for you *there*."

"I really don't have a say in it. If it's my time, it's my time." He presses those evergreen eyes into mine. "Just always remember, no matter what, I love you, Lottie Lemon. And that will never change."

My heart wrenches just hearing those words as I pull him in hard. "I love you, too, Noah. And that will never change."

Everett helps me gather another armful of the tasty pumpkin pies I've been asked to cater for the event and Noah follows along as we head inside.

The kitchen is light and bright and that's exactly where I find both Naomi and her twin, Keelie, who happens to be my very best friend.

Ironically, Naomi is a far cry from even a friend. Back in high school, she tried to steal my boyfriend, Otis *Bear* Fisher, and yet she was the only girl he wouldn't cheat on me with. And now fast-forward a million years later, we're all in our mid to late twenties and Keelie is engaged to Bear and they're very much looking forward to getting married. Lucky for Keelie, Bear has cleaned up his cheating ways and we've long since mended fences.

Keelie sashays over and helps off-load the pies onto the expansive counters.

"Geez, Lot, you've outdone yourself. You must have baked at least a hundred pies." Keelie's blonde curls are swept up and she's donned an emerald green velvet dress. Keelie is so beautiful she could be walking every runaway the world over.

"What about the whipped cream?" Naomi snaps. "Tell me you have that. There is no pumpkin pie without whipped cream."

Naomi is beautiful, too—on the outside, that is. She and Keelie are twins. But Naomi has decided to eschew her blonde locks and has dyed her tresses a striking jet-black. It only seems to sharpen her beauty and makes her all that much more stunning.

"Relax," I say. "Everett already helped me put it in the refrigerator. We'll dole out most of the pie with whipped cream and a few without. There's always someone in the crowd who doesn't want anything to do with it."

"Speaking of crowds"—Keelie ticks her head toward the ballroom next door—"have you seen the bodies lining that room? All of Honey Hollow has turned out tonight."

"All of Vermont," I counter.

Alex and Lily wander into the kitchen and both Keelie and I freeze.

"Alex, my man." Everett heads over to Alex and offers him a quick pat on the back. Alex is Noah's brother and his doppelgänger in every way, with the exception of those blowup muscles of his.

I'll admit, it's been downright painful for me to be around Alex ever since Noah's accident. He's a constant reminder that Noah isn't well enough to be out and about in the world and may never be. Alex assured me just yesterday he's still trying to get ahold of their mother. She's off on some grand worldly adventure and can't be reached. I'm sure the poor thing will be shaken when she hears about her son. That's news no mother wants to hear.

I glance around the room to look Noah's way, but I can't find him anywhere. A viral panic strikes me, and my body shakes at the thought of missing out on my chance to spend some alone time with him.

Lily speeds over. "What's the matter, Lottie? You look like you've seen a ghost." Lily Swanson is a pretty brunette who works for me down at the Cutie Pie Bakery and Cakery. I've known Lily forever. She and Naomi were the very best of friends up until a couple of months ago when Alex rode into town and tore their friendship apart without meaning to by way of dating both of them. Lily and Naomi have been warring for Alex's affection ever since and he's yet to choose which side of the estrogen fence he'd like to land on.

"No, I don't see a ghost." And that's exactly the problem.

Lily and I haven't always gotten along. Since Naomi has held a lifelong general dislike for me—due to the fact Bear wouldn't have her—Lily held the grudge as well, simply by proxy.

Alex and Everett are quickly embroiled in a heavy conversation about finance. Alex is a numbers guy, an investment banker by trade. He was in the Marines a while back, and that just seems to up his value with the ladies.

Naomi struts over to Lily, and Keelie and I gird ourselves as if a war were about to break out.

"Nice dress," Naomi says it with that dead look in her eyes, her smile tight and manufactured. "I didn't know the morgue was offering their selections to the living."

Lily gasps. "Oh yeah? How about you return that fake hair to the llama it came from? That's right." She looks to Keelie and me. "Naomi has been wearing hair extensions for years!"

Now it's Keelie and me gasping. However Naomi is getting her long luscious locks, I wouldn't beat her down over it. She has some of the best hair in Honey Hollow.

My sisters, Meg and Lainey, head into the kitchen.

Speaking of hair, Lainey and I share the same caramel-colored waves and hazel eyes. She married the love of her life last summer, a fireman by the name of Forest Donovan, and has been walking on air ever since.

Meg, much like Naomi, dyes her hair a raven's wing black. Her eyes are pale, icy blue, so the combination looks striking on her. She's dating Hook Redwood of Redwood Realty, and together they make an adorable pair. But *adorable* isn't exactly a word I'd use to describe my little sister. She's as tough as they come. She spent years on the Las Vegas female wrestling circuit under the moniker Madge the Badge. Now she teaches strippers their sultry moves down at a gentlemen's club called Red Satin.

Meg looks to Lily and Naomi and grunts, "Don't tell me it's the same old song. How could the two of you let a man destroy your friendship like that?"

Lainey scoffs. "Because he won't choose! Don't you remember when Hook was seeing both you and Keelie? The two of you weren't exactly getting along that great either."

"*Fox.*" Meg wastes no time calling Alex over. Both he and Everett look a little unnerved by Meg's harsh bark. "Pick a lane and stick to it. What you've done to these ladies isn't fair. They used to actually speak to one another, in the event you weren't aware of the fact."

Alex pumps out a dry laugh as if it were funny. "Wait. Are you serious?"

"Yes," Lainey answers for her. "They were best friends. Sure, they were a couple of mean girls, but they liked each other. But now they're just plain old mean girls."

Everett takes a breath. "I wasn't going to say anything, but they're right. You should decide who you think you mesh better with and get on with building a relationship. Unless, of course, you're not in a relationship stage of life. And if that's the case, let them know that, too."

Naomi grunts, "Of course he's in a relationship stage. We're practically there. If it weren't for the fact Lily has latched to his side like a barnacle, we'd be engaged by now."

Lily growls as if she's about to attack. But before she can get to it, a tall redhead, the district manager of the Evergreen Manor, Trisha Maples, comes in with her orange lips twisted into a serious scowl. Her hair is piled in a bun and she's wearing a crimson gown with sequin leaves sewn across the front of it, looking as festive as can be. She barrels in and begins barking at Naomi to stop navel gazing without thought as to who else might be listening to her berate her coworker.

Trisha gasps as she ogles the mountain of pumpkin pies set over the counters. "Naomi! You had better not have overestimated the dessert again. I can't have the food costs exceeding the budgeted amount. The last thing I want to do is take money from needy families just to pay for another one of your mathematical errors." She glares at the rest of us. "Dinner is being served to our guests. And the rest of you are missing your meals." She bites the words out, each its own kernel of rage, and the room drains in an instant.

Everett and I are the last to leave, and I watch as Trisha bullets past us into the ballroom.

"Now there's an angry woman. I have never seen her not worked up over something."

Everett takes a breath. "I've found people like that have a lot going on below the surface."

"Yeah, like volcanic activity."

Everett and I step into the grand ballroom and I'm blown away with all the festive decorations. Each table has a pumpkin centerpiece filled with sunflowers courtesy of my mother's horticulture club. There are bright orange maple leaves strewn into garland and hung over the walls. Dozens upon dozens of large round tables fill the enormous hall, and every familiar face in Honey Hollow seems to be here tonight, minus Noah, of course.

Even Cormack has ceased her vigil and donned a pretty rose gold dress that shimmers with her every move. She's seated at a table with Aspen and Kelleth, my newly discovered sisters.

After I found out Mayor Nash was my biological father, I gained three new siblings along with him. Finn, my brother, is seated at the table, too, with his new girlfriend, Britney.

Britney is Noah's ex-wife, which makes things a bit weird, but Britney and I have grown to be friends in the past few months. She's a franchisee of the Swift Cycle gyms and has been happily peppering them all over Vermont. She just opened one down the street from the bakery. And once the spin class is over, she has all of her members walk over to my bakery to *swiftly* replace all the calories they lost. It's a win-win for both of us.

Everett leans in. "Let's find a seat."

I'm about to lead him to the table Meg and Lainey landed at when I spot a strange swirl of light over by the front of the room. I'm about to cry out Noah's name in hopes it's him making a ghostly reprisal, but the light becomes brighter as a strange looking sight appears.

"Oh no," I moan as if I might be sick and quickly take up Everett's hand.

"What is it, Lemon?"

I give Everett's hand a squeeze. I've always adored the way he insists on calling me by my surname.

But I can't seem to answer him right now. I've been completely rendered speechless.

It is Noah I see, but he's not alone. He reappears fully in a splendid burst of light and walks over with a magnificent creature by his side. It's a gorgeous off-white llama with curly fur, a tuft of wild hair just above its forehead, a fray of bucked teeth sticking out, large coffee-colored eyes, and lashes that fan out at least three inches.

Noah smiles as he gently pats the creature's back. "I've got another one for you, Lot. You know what that means, right?"

"Lemon, what do you see?"

"A big, beautiful llama." I lean in toward its friendly face, hoping it doesn't have the sudden urge to spit. "What's your name and who's going to die?" I ask point-blank. It used to be that whenever I saw one of these ghostly creatures it meant nothing more than a minor injury, but as of late it always means an impending homicide for their previous owner.

The llama lifts its chin my way before dissolving in a spray of glorious light.

"It's gone," I whisper. "Noah, you can help us. We need to stop this murder before it ever happens."

Noah opens his mouth as if to say something, and just like that, his own body dissolves in a spiral of dazzling stars.

"I'm sorry, Lottie." His voice fades to nothing.

The din of laughter and causal dinner conversation take over once again as I look up at Everett.

"There's going to be a murder," I say in a breathless panic.

He gives a solemn nod. "Someone in this room will die tonight. What can we do to stop it?"

"Nothing."

And that's the honest truth.

2

Melee.

No sooner is the pumpkin pie delivered to each table than the masses begin to mingle. As the music grows louder and the conversations cue up at a rapid pace, pies are quickly being abandoned, and no one is requesting another single slice.

Naomi heads my way, looking completely frazzled. “Do something, Lottie. I can’t have a stitch of pie leftover. My neck is on the line. You heard my boss. She’s out for blood!”

Carlotta trots up and chortles. “Got a problem with someone? Kill ’em! With Lottie around, no one will suspect a thing. Lottie will cover for you, right?” She swats me on the arm. “Just make sure it looks like an accident.” She gives a hard wink and Naomi lets out a shout of exasperation before she takes off into the brewing crowd.

Carlotta, my birth mother, looks exactly like me, with the exception of a peppering of gray hair and wrinkles. Carlotta had me when she was just sixteen, before abandoning me on the floor of the firehouse where a kind man by the name of Joseph Lemon found me swaddled in a blanket. Carlotta left a note asking that I be named, well, Carlotta, and my mother, Miranda Lemon, was kind enough to oblige. But my mother quickly nicknamed me Lottie, and my formal name was never used.

Carlotta's eyes light up with glee. Never a good sign with this one. The things she finds glee in, other people recoil from in horror.

"Did you see her? Did you see her? About yea high, blonde, has a bodacious body." She swings her hips from side to side.

"If by *her*, you mean the haunted llama who comes bearing drama? Then yes, I saw her. Did you happen to notice who she was with?"

"Oh yes, I did. If you ask me, that naughty brat deserves a good pop to her bottom for acting the way she does."

"Wait—was Cormack anywhere near the specter scene?"

"I meant Lea." She points hard to the middle of the room and I turn to find the poor llama trotting like a racehorse while little Lea, *Azalea*—but don't you dare call her that lest she behead you, and I don't doubt she could find a way—yanks her around the dance floor. Lea is one of the three ghosts haunting my mother's bed and breakfast.

Greer Giles, a girl about my age who died last winter, has taken up residence at the B&B along with her two-hundred-year-old boyfriend, Winslow Decker. Winslow is a cutie. And Lea? Well, she's more of a fright. It turns out, Lea's entire family was slaughtered on the land that's under the B&B and she's been haunting it ever since. Lea is about six, wears a well-worn pinafore and tattered Mary Janes. She likes to wear her long dark hair combed straight over her face, and she wields a hatchet just for the fun of it.

In fact, that's exactly what she's doing right now as she does her best to behead the crowd. Boy, am I glad she's unable to pull off the feat.

As my powers increase, so have the dead's ability to move things in the material world. If Lea truly could go on a killing spree, I'm pretty sure we'd have a worldwide massacre on our hands.

"Lovely," I say. "So, did you meet her? The llama? Can she speak? What's her name?" About a few months ago, I garnered the ability to hear the dead. And now I can hear both dead people and animals alike. It's been quite a mindbender to say the least.

I spot Mom and Mayor Nash headed this way.

Carlotta leans in. "Her name is Gemma. And she's a real *gem*, if you know what I mean."

"Did she say who she belonged to? A clue maybe as to who might bite the big one?"

She tilts her head, her demeanor suddenly far too serious. "I don't suppose this would be a bad time to tell you about the pet llama you loved so much as a toddler, would it?"

"Oh you." I'm quick to wave her off. "You have no idea what I loved as a toddler. You were twelve entire states away."

"It doesn't mean I didn't wish a llama on you."

"I'm about to wish a llama on *you*."

Mom sashays up with a telling little grin. Her freshly dyed blonde curls spring over her shoulders with every step, and her fuchsia pink lips are twisted in a mischievous bow. My mother looks at least twenty years younger than her stated age, and she has a youthful vigor to match.

And just as she's almost upon us, a gray-haired ghoul pops up right next to her.

A tiny scream evicts from me as I press my hand to my chest.

"*Lottie*." Mom makes a face. "What's got you so jangled?"

"What's he doing here?" I covertly point to the aforementioned ghoul. Okay, so he's not really a ghoul. He just acts like one.

Topper Blakley is a man my mother made the mistake of entertaining until she found out he liked to entertain more than one woman at a time in his coital chambers. I helped kick him to the curb the night of that big swinger soirée he duped my mother into hosting.

She makes a face. "Relax, Lottie. Topper and I are just casual dating, as you kids like to call it." She's hopping to the music, laughing through every other word. If I didn't know better, I'd bet my mother hit the pumpkin spiced cocktails a little too hard.

Topper leans in, his gaze still set in the crowd. "Casual dating," he parrots as if he has no idea what the words mean, and I don't doubt he's clueless. Topper isn't exactly up to speed with monogamy either.

"Great." I don't bother hiding the sarcasm in my voice because Lord knows I can count on the audaciously loud music to drown it out for me.

"Oh"—Mom shakes as if we were experiencing a momentary electrocution—"before I forget, I'm going to be hosting Thanksgiving for everyone at the B&B this year. I want us all to come together as one big happy family."

"That sounds perfect." We had it at my place last year, but without Noah fully present I don't think I could pull it off.

Mayor Nash pops up on my left and blows a party horn in my face as if it were New Year's Eve, and I jump and stop breathing all at once.

"Lottie, Dottie!" he shouts with a giant grin on his face. "Are you ladies having a good time? The entire town has come out. I have a feeling we're going to exceed our fundraising goals. And if we do, I vow to make this an annual event!" Mayor Nash, aka my biological father, shares my caramel waves and olive skin. Our noses might be near identical, but it's hard to tell. The man never stops moving.

Naomi waves wildly at me. She looks particularly stabby, and if I'm not careful, a very real stabbing might occur—*mine.*

"That's wonderful," I shout. "I'd better go. It looks as if I'm needed in the kitchen."

I glance back into the crowd in search of Naomi once again, but it looks as if she's been absorbed in the sea of bodies. Instead, I come upon her boss, Trisha.

The tall redhead waves me over to the small crowd she's standing with, and I do my best not to openly cringe. I'm not sure how I'd react if she berated me in front of all these people. But, no matter how moody she might be, I would still like to have a working relationship with the Evergreen Manor. In other words, I'm more than willing to grin and bear it.

She pulls me in and slings her arm over my shoulders. "Everyone, this is the fabulous baker who made those pies we've all been raving about."

The four faces all poised my way, three women and a man, offer up a myriad of accolades.

"Thank you. It's my sweet grandmother Nell's recipe. She was the owner of the Honey Pot Diner. So if you ever want to stop by, they'll be serving my pumpkin pies right through Christmas. And, of course, my shop, the Cutie Pie Bakery and Cakery, is right next door and we serve them up, too." And when Nell passed away, she not only left me half of Honey Hollow, including the Honey Pot Diner, but she bequeathed to me her sweet cat Waffles, a brother to my own cat Pancake. They're both gorgeous fluffy Himalayans with silver-blue eyes.

The older woman has her frayed gray hair slicked into a chignon. She looks wide-eyed and very interested, and I recognize that hungry gleam. She's calculating exactly how many pies she'll need.

"Do you take orders?" she's quick to inquire.

"I sure do. But put it in quickly if you plan to. It can get tricky the closer we get to Thanksgiving."

"Sure thing." She looks to the younger girl next to her. She's about my age with dark copper hair piled on top of her head. Her skin is a rich shade of almond and the string of pearls around her neck glow ethereal. She has on a fitted cherry red dress with long brown boots that hit over the knee, and I can't help but admire them. "We'll do that next week. That way, we won't have to worry about burning the pies like we did last year."

The young woman rolls her eyes. "The holidays will thankfully never be the same."

Trisha chortles. "Lottie, this is my friend Gerrie and her niece Annette. Gerrie and I volunteer together down at the shelter in Leeds— where I'm in charge of the volunteers, of course. Gerrie couldn't handle the position."

Gerrie's eyes grow wild as she looks my way. "This woman is a troublemaker." Her voice shakes as if she were viscerally angry with her.

I try my best to laugh it off. "I'm sure she does it to keep you on your toes."

The younger girl, the bronze model, glowers at Trisha a moment before stepping over and whispering something into her ear before yanking her aunt into the crowd.

Trisha straightens. She looks visibly shaken, batting her lashes as if fighting a burst of emotions herself.

I glance at the man and the woman left in our circle before leaning toward Trisha.

"Are you okay?" I can't help but ask. That wasn't just awkward to witness, I can tell whatever Annette just whispered to her stung.

Trisha waves it off. "Never mind them." She points to the older man who's quite good looking—a full head of short silver hair, a matching peppering of stubble over his well-tanned cheeks, and light eyes that have a sparkle of mischief to them. "Lottie, I'd like for you to meet my main squeeze."

Her main squeeze? He looks markedly younger than her, but I say more power to her. He's older still, but you can tell he's aging well, much like the way I suspect Everett will. And Noah, too. But at this point, I'll take Noah aging badly just so long as he gets to do it.

He grunts my way, "Don't you worry about this old girl. Trisha Maples is made of steel." He extends a hand my way. "Leo Workman. I'm Trisha's steady Eddie."

The young girl next to him with long dark hair and pale glowing skin waves over to me. "And I'm Jade. I'm her assistant." She glances off into the crowd a moment.

"It's nice to meet you both," I say before reverting my attention to Trisha. "I'll go make sure there's plenty more pie for those who want it." I nod to the three of them before taking off.

No sooner do I hit the exit than I hear little Lea shrieking with joy, and I turn in time to see her galloping poor Gemma up to the makeshift stage.

I'm about to head to the kitchen again when I spot Leo Workman dragging Trisha off in haste and she doesn't look too sorry about it. I bet he's got more Everett in him than I gave him credit for. A body crashes into mine and we bounce off of one another like rubber balls. It's Jade, the assistant I just met.

"So sorry," she says, patting the air between us. Her eyes are a tangle of crimson tracks, and I wonder how I could have missed that a moment ago. "Excuse me." She takes off running down the hall and out the back exit.

"So strange," I say as I push my way past the crowd in an effort to help Naomi hide those pies.

She over ordered. Of course she did.

Trisha is right. I tried to warn Naomi, but she assured me she needed every pie she asked for. And I did deliver—much to both our chagrin at the moment.

"Excuse me." A woman with long red hair, glowing pale skin, and bee-stung lips that I would die for knocks her shoulder to mine. "Can anyone go in there?" She's eyeing the bar just inside the venue.

"Oh sure. Dinner is over. I'm sure they won't mind if you pop in." I muster an affable smile. She's probably a guest of the manor. I would never say no to a customer. "Have a great time."

"I will." Her eyes slit to nothing. She brushes past me, nearly taking my shoulder out with her.

"Geez." I glare in her direction, only to watch as she sneaks her way right to the bar and snatches an entire bottle off the counter before disappearing into the crowd. "Oh, that was low." I groan as I make my way to the kitchen to find Naomi scowling. "Well, I've just lost my faith in humanity."

Naomi glowers at me—her go-to look. "Well, I've just lost my job."

"Oh, please tell me you're kidding," I say, stacking the enormous surplus of pies upon one another so they'll be easier to carry.

"I'm kidding, but I won't be for long. I'll help you throw these away."

"Are you insane? I'm not throwing these pies away. This is perfectly good food. I'm driving them down to the shelter in Leeds—courtesy of the Evergreen Manor, of course, since you did pay for them."

She scoffs. "Trisha is right. I'm not a numbers girl."

"So what? Next time give me the expected head count, and I promise you won't have too much or too little of anything."

Naomi starts tossing pies into a heap as haphazardly as she can, and I'm quick to ward her off.

"Hold your fire! Look, just do me a favor and go find Everett. He won't mind helping, and I can really use his muscles."

"I know what you can use his muscles for." She gives a sly wink. "You want to get the holidays started off on the right thrust, and I can't say I blame you." She takes off before I can correct her.

"*Please*"—I mutter as I carry a stack of pies out the back door and into the icy fall air—"I can have Everett anytime I want. I certainly don't need to pull him away from a conversation he's enjoying just to have my way with him." It's true. He's been talking to Hook and Alex all night about the investment company they're looking to start up.

"Good to hear," a deep voice rumbles from my right. I nearly chuck all of the pies out of my arms and into the starry night.

"Whoa!" Noah flies right through me in an effort to stabilize them.

"It's you." I sigh with relief. "You're not only a sight for sore eyes, you're a sight for sore muscles. Would you mind?"

"Not at all. Hand 'em over."

I slide the heft of them into his arms.

Noah blows out a breath he doesn't need. "I'd do anything to take a bite out of one. These smell fantastic."

"Sorry about that. So, have you been to paradise? The others are very elusive about it, but I'm *dying* to know what it's like." I wrinkle my nose at him. "Not the wording I was looking for. Sorry."

"Don't be. I'm as dead as can be, and I haven't seen it yet."

"That's because you're not dead—enough."

I open the van and help Noah shove the pies inside.

A shuffling sound emits from the left and we both hold our breath a moment—not that Noah needs his next breath at all.

A blonde in a rose gold gown giggles as she heads for the woods with a man by her side.

I suck in a quick breath, "Noah, I think that's Cormack."

"What?" He squints over at them. "Who's that guy?"

"I don't know. Maybe head over and spy on them. If she's in trouble, come back and tell me. I'll get help."

His dimples dig in deep. "We make a great team whether or not I'm in the land of the living." He lands a light kiss to my lips, and I shiver at the strange sensation.

Noah takes off just as Everett comes down the walk with his arms laden with pies.

"Rumor has it, we have a very hot date in the icy woods." His brows bounce with the innuendo.

"I'd say yes, but Cormack beat us to it. How about we build a fire at my place afterwards and we can—" A full-blown argument erupts to our right and throws off my train of thought. "My word, that's pretty heated."

The sound of a woman pleading or *screaming* eats up the night, followed by a distinct pop.

"Oh my goodness." I grip Everett and he's quick to pull me in.

"That was a gunshot."

"I'll say."

We head toward the building, carefully making our way around the corner to see if we can spot anything—like a madman with a gun.

Out in the parking lot, in between a dense population of cars, a piece of fabric shimmers on the ground.

I glance back at Everett. "See that?" I point over to it. "It looks like a scarf or a purse." I start to head out and Everett pulls me in close to him.

"Not without me," he whispers.

We edge our way over and a breath gets caught in my throat.

"That's no scarf," I whimper as we crest the row of parked cars to see it for what it really is. "That's human hair."

Red hair.

Everett and I take a step closer and my heart sinks once I see that all too familiar face.

Naomi doesn't have to worry about being fired tonight.

Trisha Maples can't fire another soul ever again.

Trisha Maples is dead.

3

A shrill scream drills from my throat.

Lying prone in the street with a slice of my pumpkin pie spilled over her chest is poor Trisha Maples with her auburn hair splayed out, a trickle of blood around the glossy wound blooming over her heart.

"*Lottie*!" Noah swoops our way, panting as if he needed to, but I suspect it's more out of habit than anything else. "Text Ivy. I'll scan the periphery." He zooms off, zipping around the dark parking lot like a pale blue flash of lightning. "Keep Everett with you," his voice echoes unnaturally loud.

"Come on, Lemon"—Everett tries to pull me along—"we need to get help. And I'm not leaving you out here."

"Noah said to text Ivy, but my fingers can't seem to behave," I pant the words out at my phone in a fit of frustration.

Everett shoots off a text for me, and within a moment Detective Ivy Fairbanks, Noah's homicide investigation partner down at the Ashford County Sheriff's Department, strides out in a long brown coat and a pair of pointed black stilettos. Ivy is a leggy redheaded stunner, and I've always suspected she had a crush on Noah. And how I hate framing that in the past tense.

"Get back," Ivy barks at the two of us as she heads over to check for vitals. "The killer could still be at large." She fiddles with her phone, and soon every deputy and fireman inside the Evergreen Manor drains into the parking lot.

Soon enough, the area is cordoned off and several more patrol cars are screaming their way through the night.

Noah zooms back, and I take up Everett's hand.

"What did you see, Noah?"

"A shoe." His glowing green eyes glance to the scene of the crime. "Tell Ivy there's a high heel near the exit on the left side of the building. That's all I found. A shoe."

I bolt over and shout for Ivy, flagging her down before the owner of that shoe comes back and ruins Noah's big find.

"Ivy!" I call out and she hooks those angry eyes of hers on mine.

"What?" she hisses as she stalks my way. "I'm in the middle of an investigation. This had better be important."

"It is, I swear. Noah said he found a shoe outside on the rear exit."

She takes a breath and softens a notch. "You mean Everett. You said Noah." She gives a long blink. "I'll have one of the deputies check it out as soon as they can."

"Oh, they need to do it now. What if it's gone? What if the shoe belongs to the killer? I mean, if it does, it's obviously a woman, right? And Everett and I heard arguing and then a scream and a gunshot."

Her pointed brows pinch together. "Did you see anything?"

"No, not a thing. We just came out to see what was happening and there she was." My hand claps over my mouth. "Just lying there on the ground all alone."

Ivy averts her eyes as if she's not buying the emotion I'm dishing out.

"Very good, Lottie. I'll consider that your official statement. I have good news and I have bad news for you."

Everett steps over, panting as if he just jogged a long way.

"What is it? I want it all," I ask, breathless myself.

Ivy curls her lips at both Everett and me. "The good news is, I'm able to release your gun back into your custody from last month's debacle. Now that the investigation is over, we no longer need to hold it in evidence."

"Yes," I cheer quietly as I shoot Everett a brief look of glee. "I can't wait to have Ethel back. That's what I named her," I tell Ivy. "She's special. It's the gun Noah and Everett bought me to protect myself."

She closes her eyes and nods once again. "I understand."

"And the bad news?" I'm almost afraid to ask.

"The bad news is, you don't get to putz around in my investigation."

Noah crops up behind her looking less than pleased—although I've lost track of how many times he's said the same thing to me.

A plume of fog expels from Ivy's nostrils and gives her a fire breathing dragon appeal.

"Now that Noah isn't here, I think we need some firm ground rules." Her jaw stiffens. "Please bear in mind they are strictly for your benefit. You are a civilian, Lottie. On occasion, I feared that Detective Fox had lost sight of that fact."

"Hardly," Noah grunts.

"Nevertheless"—she continues—"you're to abstain from every aspect of this case. And if I find you tampering with my evidence or my suspects, I won't hesitate to have you arrested." She shoots a sharp look to Everett. "That goes for you, too, Judge Baxter. I'm guessing it wouldn't be the first time the two of you have been in handcuffs together. Have a good rest of the night. If I need either one of you, I know where to find you." She struts back to the scene of the crime just as the coroner's van rolls into the parking lot.

"She's a battleax," I say.

"She's right," both Noah and Everett chime in unison.

Everett tips his head at the airspace Noah is currently occupying, but he can't see him so it's just a pretty good guess on his part.

Everett's chest thumps. "I don't think it's any coincidence that we can finally agree on things now that you're all but gone."

"*Everett*," I'm quick to scold. "Behave."

"I'm telling the truth. I meant no offense."

Noah gives a wistful shake of the head. "And I take no offense to it. Everett specializes in the truth, Lottie. And I not only appreciate it, I happen to agree with him."

"Noah, what about Cormack? Is she okay?"

He averts his eyes. "She's with some guy."

"What guy?"

"I'm afraid to tell you."

"Tell me, now."

Everett's chest bounces. "You'd better tell her, Noah, or she just might kill you."

"Funny." Noah leans in and presses those glowing green eyes my way. "She was with Topper Blakley."

"What?" I squawk so loud, half the deputies turn my way. "Cormack was with Grandpa Jones? What in the heck was she doing with him?"

Noah's brows bounce. "What wasn't she doing with him?"

"Oh." I suck in a never-ending breath. "*Eww*!"

The deputies ask us to clear the area, and I'm about to tell them I'm related to the man who wears the shiny badge. Keelie's father, Jack, is the sheriff himself. But Everett navigates me toward the building before I can get to it.

"Oh dear!" a woman's voice emits from the side and we pause a moment as the sound of hoof beats prance in this direction. "I've missed it, haven't I?" That luscious llama bounds over, batting her long lashes so fast I'd swear I could feel the breeze of a hurricane.

"Gemma." Noah motions the magnificent beast over with a tick of his head. "Come meet Lottie." He looks to me, suddenly filled with concern. "Is Toby okay?"

Toby is Noah's Golden Retriever that he shares custody of with his ex-wife.

"Britney's staying at your place with him." I offer a guilty shrug.

"*And*?" Noah senses something is up, I can tell.

"And my new brother, Finn, is staying there with her."

Noah gives an audible groan as if someone just kicked him below the belt.

Everett's lips twitch. "If it means anything to you, Finn complains that he hates the shower. He says there's not enough room for two."

Noah offers him a disparaging look.

Finn is wrong, by the way. There is plenty of room for two. You just need to know how to work it. Noah and I have managed it on quite a few occasions, thank you very much.

Everett could fit half the bakery in his amply spacious shower. Just saying.

Gemma trots up, panting as if she just circled all of Honey Hollow.

"I just ran a lap around the entire building." She elongates the last word until it sounds as if she's braying. "My apologies. I'm afraid I'm not used to being earthbound anymore. And I haven't figured out how to come and go around here. What's happened? Who died?"

Everett glances in her general vicinity. "Trisha Maples. Someone shot her in the parking lot."

The panting poltergeist seems to stagger on all four feet. "Oh goodness! Not Trisha. This is terrible! Somebody do something! Someone call the police!"

I comb my fingers through her fur and marvel at how soft she feels. "The sheriff's department is already here, Gemma. Don't worry. They're doing everything they can." Gemma is so sweet with that puff of frayed white hair sitting on top of her head, those adorable—albeit severely bucked teeth—I just want to land a kiss on her velvet nose.

Everett holds his phone between us and pulls up a picture. "Noah found a shoe."

"Everett, I can't believe you took a picture of that shoe! Good work."

"I figured I'd better do it while you and Ivy were speaking. I had a feeling we'd head in this direction."

I pull his phone forward and inspect it. "Were you ever right. Hey? It's a picture of a dark navy stiletto with a gold band over the toe. Not a shoe you'd see every day. I bet if we go back inside, we might find someone holding her other shoe."

Noah looks back to the rear of the building as Ivy heads that way with a couple of deputies.

"Come with me, Gemma," he says. "I'll teach you a few tricks." They zoom off together, and Everett and I head back inside. We make our way into the grand ballroom once again and are immediately accosted by my mother.

"Lottie!" Her face is bright red, her eyes filled with rage. "Meg says she saw Topper leaving the building with some blonde tart. Say it's not so. Did you see him out there?"

The music is so boisterously loud, the bodies only seem to have multiplied, and it's thick with humidity in here compared to the icy air outdoors.

"Actually"—I shoot Everett a nervous glance—"I didn't *see* anything." There. In no way do I want to open a can of Cormack Featherby worms.

Lainey and Meg run up, wild-eyed, with Hook Redwood tagging along behind them. Hook is Meg's official plus one. He's tall, has a head full of wavy brown hair, and prior to moving back to Honey Hollow, he made Wall Street his stomping grounds. He's as sharp as they come.

Lainey grabs me by the shoulders. "Forest just let me know there's been another murder. Tell me you had nothing to do with it."

"Of course, I had nothing to do with it."

Meg snorts. "Did you find the body?"

My mouth opens, but not a word comes out.

Lainey stomps her heel. "Oh, Lottie. That's it! I'm going to find somebody who is qualified to take this curse off you."

"I'm not cursed, far from it."

Lily trots up with Alex in tow.

"What were they eating, Lottie?" Lily leans in with such intensity I'm half-afraid she'll fall onto me.

I let out a hard sigh. "Pumpkin pie."

Lily pulls out her phone. "I'll get right on it."

Mom snaps her fingers. "Good thinking! And I'll make sure to tell all my Haunted Honey Hollow tourists what to expect. Ooh, that pumpkin pie was so delicious. I think it's that extra dash of nutmeg." She gives a little wink.

"It's the extra splash of vanilla," I counter.

And it's true. My mother has no qualms about profiting from the dead and the living alike. Now that her B&B is fully infested with poltergeists, she's charging eighty dollars a pop for tourists to come and ogle the bevy of floating objects and the books that suspiciously knock themselves from the shelves. And once they're good and spooked, she ships them off my way for what she's dubbed The Last Thing They Ate Tour. Sadly, it's a financial gain for both of us.

Lainey shakes her head. "I'll fix this for you, Lottie. I don't know how, but I will."

I bite down hard on my lip. I don't know why I've never confided in my sisters about my supersensual standing, but I haven't.

"Oh!" Lainey lifts a finger. "Before I forget, could you drop by one night this week? Forest's family is having Thanksgiving early because one of his sisters has to go to her in-laws' house on the big day, and they asked me to bake the pies. Could you teach me?"

"Are you kidding? I would love to. Meg, you should come too. We'll do a little sister bonding. And you, too, Mom." Now that she's down a man in her life, I'm afraid of what she'll do if left to her own devices.

Naomi runs up, her face as pale as the linen tablecloths set out all around us.

"Lottie, is it true? You killed Trisha Maples?"

"What? *No*. I don't know who killed her. Someone shot her. I'm so sorry, Naomi."

"Are you kidding? It's the best news I've had all night. Ding-dong! The witch is dead. I'd better contact the higher-ups. It looks as if I'm about to get my old position back." She takes off before I can scold her from emitting too much glee.

Hook offers to take Meg, Lainey, and Mom home and we indulge in one big group hug before they take off.

Everett and I quickly busy ourselves by looking for the navy high heel with a gold tip but to no avail. Whoever wore those shoes here tonight has long taken off. And we can't even be sure she was the killer.

The music switches to something softer, something sad, and Everett pulls me into his arms.

"What are you doing?" I ask sweetly as I cross my wrists behind his neck.

Everett begins to sway our bodies to the rhythm, and soon enough we're doing the unthinkable—dancing.

"I just think you need to catch a break, Lemon, and I want to be the one who gives it to you."

"You just melted my heart," I say as he bows in and lands a tender kiss to my forehead. Everett spins me slowly and I delight in the dizzy feeling that makes me want to close my eyes forever. And when I blink back to life, my heart gives a sharp wallop once I spot Noah watching from across the room. His glowing green eyes are feasted right over us, and before I can move or blink, he disappears to nothing.

It doesn't feel fair.

It doesn't feel right.

Not only did we stumble upon a murder, it feels as if Everett and I just killed Noah.

Everett is right.

I need to catch a break. We all do.

But first, I think I'll defy Detective Fairbanks' wishes and catch a killer.

4

Honey Hollow is in the thick of autumn—i.e., leaf peeping season.

The entire town is bursting at the seams with tourists who have come up to witness the autumn wonderland our little corner of Vermont has transformed into. My mother's B&B is booked solid, but the ghosts have more to do with it than the leaves.

However, I have no idea how the Evergreen Manor is doing now that there's been another murder on their grounds. The only person happy about that grisly fact is Naomi. Keelie let me know this morning that Naomi won't have to worry about another district manager for a while. The company is in the middle of a hiring freeze. I'll have to stop by some time and talk to Naomi about what happened—get her take on things.

If Ivy thinks she's pushing me out of this investigation, she's as delusional as Cormack is with Noah. I need to start compiling my suspect list and I'll need Naomi's help with that.

Lily leans in with a carafe of our pumpkin spiced coffee in her hand. "I think Naomi did it."

I roll my eyes.

"What?" She decides to play coy. "I could tell you were thinking about it. I've known you long enough to recognize that look."

She's right. There's no way I can fight her on that.

It's just past noon and the Cutie Pie Bakery and Cakery has already had its fair share of customers. Lily and I have been working nonstop for the last four hours, so this tiny lull in confection-fueled traffic feels like a respite. And, of course, she's using it to implicate her ex-best friend in a murder. Things really hit the fan between the two of them once Naomi discovered that Lily is actually bedding their shared boyfriend.

"Lily, we both know Naomi didn't do it. She doesn't know how to fire a gun, let alone own one."

"We don't truly know that about her. I didn't know *you* owned a gun up until a few weeks ago, and here you've been harboring a concealed weapon all along."

"That reminds me. I need to make a trip to the sheriff's department to pick her up. Boy, do I ever miss Ethel." Ethel is the Glock that Noah and Everett teamed up to buy me.

Noah also gave me shooting lessons. He has such a big and thoughtful heart and all he ever wanted to do was give it all to me.

I press my lips tight to keep from spontaneously weeping—a phenomenon that Lily is all too familiar with by now.

"Lottie"—Lily rubs my back—"go see him. That always makes you feel better."

"Wow, you really do know what I'm thinking. You can't read minds, can you?"

A laugh bubbles from her. "Only your face. You're like an open book."

"Well, you're wrong about me feeling better when I see Noah. I feel worse. I don't know what I'll do if he dies, Lily," I whisper the words in the event Noah's ghost decides to pop up at an inopportune moment.

"If he does kick the bucket, it's probably in an effort to get away from Cormack."

"Do you know she's been there every single day?"

"So have you."

"Yeah, but I'm not posting selfies of us to every social media site."

She whips out her phone. "Huh. Looks like Cormack hasn't hit the hospital yet this afternoon."

"Give her time." My lips twitch because I happen to be holding back some serious Featherby gossip.

Lily's eyes grow large. "What is it, Lottie? It looks as if you're about to explode if you don't tell me what's on your mind."

I make a face. I'm still not ruling out the mind reading thing.

"Fine. But don't say a word." I lean in. "Cormack was spotted trotting off into the woods with that weirdo my mother was seeing."

She gasps. "Brad Rutherford? Rich Dallas? Mayor Nash? Pastor Gaines? Which weirdo, Lottie? Which one?"

"I'm staggeringly impressed that you've memorized my mother's lineup of weirdos. But none of the above—and besides, two of them are dead."

"That's because you killed one."

It's true. Last month I was forced to do the unthinkable and I cracked a stick over Pastor Gaines' temple and killed him. I'd like to think it wouldn't have happened if he weren't trying to kill me first. But then, he was doing some pretty shady things, and my mother was next in line to get a full serving of shady dished out by the dicey pastor.

"It's Topper Blakley," I whisper and Lily sucks up all the oxygen in the room.

"Oh my goodness! How could you have kept this from me? This is too good." She whips out her phone and spins around as she begins manically typing away.

"Lily! You just said you wouldn't say anything!"

"I'm not saying anything! I'm writing." She trots off to the kitchen just as the door chimes and another slew of customers head in.

"You were saved by the bell, Lily," I say as I quickly help every last one of them out.

The pumpkin spiced cake, pumpkin cheesecake, pumpkin cinnamon rolls, and, of course, the pumpkin pies have been flying off the shelves. I don't know how the farmers on this planet produce enough pumpkins to satisfy everyone's cravings this time of year. And I've already had enough advanced pie orders, both pecan and the aforementioned peachy globe, to keep me busy the entire week leading up to Thanksgiving—that is, if I bake nonstop.

I steal a moment to look around.

The Cutie Pie has been mine now for one solid year. I take in the butter yellow walls and the pastel mix and match tables and chairs. There's an opening on the left side of the bakery that connects us directly to the Honey Pot Diner. And in the middle of the Honey Pot, there's a large resin oak tree whose branches crawl up over the ceiling and expand all the way into the café portion of my bakery. Each and every branch is intertwined with twinkle lights, and the effect provides a magical appeal. There's nothing else I'd rather be doing, not one other job on earth that I'm more suited for than this one right here.

A couple of familiar faces walk through the door, and I cringe, hoping this conversation doesn't take a turn for the cheating.

I force a smile in their direction. "Hey, Mom—Carlotta." For once I'm thrilled to have Carlotta here as a buffer. If my mom brings up Topper, we can deflect and change the subject. Carlotta's favorite topic is herself, so that should be easy enough.

"Hello, Lottie." Mom shoves a fistful of dollars into my tip jar because she knows it's against my policy to accept any form of legal tender from her or my sisters.

Instead of a purse, she has a bulky tote bag cinched over her shoulder and I'm mildly curious as to its contents.

"Don't you fret." She waves another fistful of dollars she plucks from her purse and repeats the action. "And don't you deny me the pleasure of being a mother. It's a mother's job to spoil her children. You'll see when you're a mother one day, Lottie. The minute you look into your beautiful baby's eyes, you'll see the reward of a lifetime."

"Hey, Lot." Carlotta smacks her lips. "You're the reward that keeps on giving. I'll take my pumpkin pinwheels for free, thank you very much."

"I'm keeping a running tab for you," I tease, quickly handing her a pinwheel.

Carlotta offers a smarmy grin and every alarm bell I have goes off at once. "Your mom and I were just taking bets on who Topper is cheating on her with."

I suck in a quick breath and shake my head at her.

Mom rolls her eyes. "We were not taking bets, Carlotta. I simply said I bet it's not someone I know."

Carlotta grunts, "It's always someone you know. Ain't that right, Lot?"

My mind rifles back to high school where I just so happened to know each and every girl Bear cheated on me with. And let's not forget Curt, my short-lived college fiancé who helped himself to my roommate of all people.

"Maybe, maybe not. Besides, what's the big deal?" I shrug over at my mother. "It's not like you were with him. Chalk it up to a bad date and move on."

"Move on?" Carlotta looks incensed by this. "And who do you purport she moves on with? My Harry?" Her voice hikes a notch as she turns to my mother. "You can't move on with my Harry."

Harry as in Harry Nash, my bio dad. It's sort of an anomaly that he's seeing Carlotta again after all these years. Most kids would be thrilled to have their parents back together, but since I didn't grow up with either of them, I'm completely indifferent to the situation.

Mom scoffs. "I'll have a pumpkin spiced latte and a chocolate croissant, please."

Lily lifts a hand. "I got this, Lot."

"Double for me," Carlotta shouts.

"Mom, you're not still seeing Topper, right?"

My mother's shoulders pin to her ears. "Don't judge me. He invited me to dinner and, of course, I said yes."

"Of course?" I balk. "Mom, I'm baffled by this. Why in the world would you go out with a man who you're certain has already cheated on you?"

Her pretty blue eyes widen. "How else am I supposed to win him back?"

Carlotta and I exchange a quick glance.

Anytime Carlotta and I appear to be on the same page about anything, I realize all is not right with the world.

Mom waves the two of us off. "I'm heading to the Scarlett Sage Boutique to pick up a snazzy little number that he won't be able to resist."

"Mom"—I choke as I try to get every protest out of me at once. "It's not you he has a problem resisting. It's other women."

She looks to the ceiling for a span of three seconds, something she would do when I was growing up just as she was about to change the subject. I always wondered if the ceiling gave her a clue on what to say next.

"Anyway"—she begins—"I hope you don't mind me being here for a while. I'm working on a book. And like every good writer, I must find a café to be my muse. I choose this one, Lottie. So, keep the tackling fuel coming." She lifts her latte my way and gives a sly wink.

Carlotta takes a breath. "Why in heaven's name are you taking pen to paper?"

"Oh, I brought my laptop. Nobody writes a novel on a legal pad, Carlotta. You might as well be writing hieroglyphics in a cave somewhere."

Speaking of caves, I wonder who's minding the haunted inn? Most likely a skeleton crew, and let's not forget the ghosts.

Mom leans in. "Before Stephen died"—her hand flies to her chest—"God rest his soul. He encouraged me to write my heart's song."

"I remember," I say. "He encouraged you to write a murder mystery on how to kill your boyfriend because he was trying to pin you for his supposed death."

She waves me off again. "I'm writing a murder mystery on how to kill your boyfriend because I'm working through some heavy distrust issues right now, Lottie. And they do say writing is cheaper than therapy."

Carlotta sniffs. "When you get to the part about cracking the dirty cheat's skull with a tree branch, be sure to ask Lottie to check for accuracy."

Mom gags on her words before gathering her coffee and croissant and speeding to a corner by the window.

Carlotta postures. "Do you think I should head down to the Scarlett Sage Boutique and pick up some snazzy duds myself?"

"Why? Do you want to date Topper, too?"

She makes a face. "Because I plan on having Harry and me bump into those lovebirds tonight, and I want to look good for our surprise double date."

"Good idea. Make sure to irritate Topper good and hard so that he'll want nothing to do with my mother and her nutty friends. The nerve of that moron for ditching into the woods with Cormack Featherby of all people. She's like a plague on our family."

Carlotta sucks in a breath at the revelation, and I do the same, realizing my grave gossip-based Featherby error.

"Don't you dare," I hiss at her, and her eyes light up like pinwheels on fire.

"I'm always up for a good dare, Lottie." Carlotta trots off to the table with my mother and I keep an eye on them for the better half of the afternoon.

A part of me keeps watch at the door, too, just hoping Noah will walk right through it. Or I suppose he could walk right through the window or the wall.

How I miss him—even if I *have* seen him in his ghostly form.

I miss him so much it hurts.

5

Lainey's new house on Maple Leaf Drive is exactly two blocks east from where I live on Country Cottage Road.

When Noah and I were seeing one another, I just fell in love with the street he lived on. So, when I was in need of a rental, and a house came available across the street from his adorable little cabin, I quickly snapped it up. And as fate and Everett's wily ways would have it, he purchased the house next to mine and we've been a happy little trifecta of angst ever since.

The house that Lainey and Forest bought is gorgeous. It's been newly renovated inside from top to bottom and has a cheery red front door to greet guests like me. She's hung a gorgeous fall wreath on it with artificial citrine-colored maple leaves and tiny little pumpkins dotting its surface.

How I love this time of year and all its spectacular décor. I'll be the first to admit, I'm a sucker when it comes to buying up all the fall-inspired decorations, and don't get me started on the nineteen boxes marked *Christmas* up in my attic.

Lainey opens the door before I can knock and pulls me into an enthusiastic embrace as I head on into her toasty warm home.

"Oh, it's heavenly in here," I say, taking off my heavy pea coat and scarf. "It's about to hit freezing tonight. Can you believe it? At this rate, we'll have snow for Thanksgiving."

Lainey groans as she leads me to the kitchen. "I know. And Forest is at the firehouse, so I don't have anyone to keep me warm tonight. But don't worry. I'm not afraid to crank that heater when Forest isn't around."

I can't help but laugh. Our dad was notoriously known as the heater police. It sounds as if Lainey chose a man just like dear old dad. And if she did, she's lucky. Other than the heating offense, Joseph Lemon was a saint.

Lainey's new house boasts an open concept floor plan with a great room that flows right into a huge kitchen, complete with a marble island and top-of-the-line appliances.

Her hair is in a perky ponytail and she already has an apron strapped to her chest that reads *A Woman Belongs in the House—and the Senate.*

"I can't do an early snowfall, though." She shudders at the thought. "You know how much I hate it when it gets icy."

"You're not alone in that. I nearly broke a leg on my own porch last winter. So how is it working out with Forest at the firehouse on and off?"

She makes a face. "I never thought being married to a fireman would be this hard, Lot. Our own dad was a firefighter for Pete's sake. We never missed him so much we thought we'd go crazy. But that's exactly how I feel. I have no idea how I'm going to get through a lifetime of this."

"I'm so sorry! If it helps, I'll come over every now and again and we'll have slumber parties."

She tosses an apron my way. "Thanks for the offer, but you snore."

"Very funny," I say, tying on the bright red Mrs. Claus apron she just chucked my way. "Remind me to get you a few plain aprons for Christmas. I have an entire box at the bakery."

"I don't want a plain apron. I like my fancy aprons. And back to your snoring. You should really do something about it. I'm surprised your boyfriends haven't complained."

"Now you're pushing it," I say, pulling forward all the ingredients she's already set out. The entire island is cluttered with everything we'll need to make the perfect pumpkin pie. I'm so thrilled to be teaching my big sis how to bake, I could just cry—or gloat. It's not often that I'm better at something than Lainey. "Go ahead and preheat the oven to four twenty-five. We're going to make up the crust and I'll teach you how to blind bake it, which just means baking it a bit so it doesn't get mushy." I set my purse down and put my hair into a quick ponytail myself. "If you don't mind, I'm going to run to the restroom real quick. All those pumpkin spiced lattes are catching up with me."

"Sure thing."

I speed off for the restroom just outside the grand room. Lainey's new house is the perfect home to build a family in. It has more than enough bedrooms to hold as many kids as they could want. And seeing that my mother badgers my poor sister for grandkids every chance she gets, I'm not even going to broach the subject tonight unless she brings it up first. Lainey mentioned to me a few weeks back that they weren't necessarily trying to have a baby, but they weren't stopping it either. Selfishly, I can't wait to hold Lainey's little cherub in my arms. It's going to be a real treat having a baby in the family.

The bathroom is just as beautifully remodeled as the kitchen with its matching marble countertop and gold-framed mirror. She even has it decorated for fall with auburn towels and a tiny pumpkin dotting the sink. I'm about to get down to business when I see there's no toilet paper.

"Nothing to bother Lainey about," I mutter as I open the cabinet under the sink and spot several new rolls calling my name. I pluck one out and knock down a stack of lavender boxes, spilling them at my feet. I pick one up. "At home pregnancy test. Early response." Oh my goodness.

I quickly restack the boxes where they belong, only to find out that there's a virtual sea of them in here. Lainey must have bought out an entire big box store. She must really be going through these if she felt she needed this many. By the looks of things, Lainey is trying a little bit harder than she's letting on.

I'm about to put back the last box when I pull it forward to inspect it instead.

"Look at this," I whisper as I open it up to find a foil wrapped test kit inside.

When was *my* last cycle? I mean, Noah and I did take our surprise marriage pretty seriously no thanks to all that closure talk Everett pushed on us. Okay, so it wasn't entirely Everett's fault.

And Noah and I weren't always that careful either. Noah was insatiable—okay, so I was a bit insatiable, too. But only because my body happened to miss his body due to the unexpected hiatus his wife forced us to take.

A wave of emotion pulses through me.

I couldn't be.

Could I?

"I guess there's only one way to find out."

There are so many tests here, I doubt Lainey would notice if one were missing.

I quickly do the deed as per the instructions and set the small plastic stick behind a tiny pumpkin on the sink that she has set out as a decoration.

I'll be back in a bit to check on it. Every muscle in my body trembles at what the results might be.

Lainey and I bake our hearts out. We talk about everything under the sun, about Meg, our mother—about Cormack. Yes, I told her about Topper. How could I not?

"She is such a skank!" Lainey wields her whisk like a weapon. "Poor Noah. It makes me feel as if she were merely using him that whole time she pretended to be obsessed with him. I mean, if you can't remain faithful while the man you're in love with is in the hospital, you have a real problem. Except for you, Lot. It would be totally understandable of you to fly into Everett's arms for comfort. Meg told me he was spending the night."

I gasp.

It's true. Everett has been spending the night ever since the day of the accident.

"We haven't done anything, you know, physical." My lips press tight as if maybe I were omitting the truth. "He's simply comforting me. It's nice. He makes me breakfast while I shower in the morning. I'm afraid he's spoiling me."

"Ah-huh." She glances at me briefly while gathering the used bowls and measuring cups from the island. "And I suppose it's nice waking up in those strong legal eagle arms in the morning, isn't it?"

I choke on my response. “Why are you judging me?”

“I knew it!” She breaks out into hysterics. “You’re sleeping in the same bed!”

“Lainey”—I try to swat her with a dishtowel, but she’s too far for me to properly dole out the punishment—“Everett happens to have a trick back. He can’t sleep on the couch and the bed in the guestroom is a twin. His legs would fall off the sides. Besides, he’s no stranger to my bed. And before you imply anything, I was telling the truth. We’re keeping it G. Noah is our priority. Everett is very respectful of our marriage.”

Lainey chortles up a storm. “He sure has a funny way of showing it. I bet he’s having fun playing house.” She trots off. “Hang on. I have something for you. I’ll be right back.”

Thoughts of Everett run through my mind so I text him.

At Lainey’s. Just finished up teaching her how to bake pies. I’m bringing a warm one home for you.

He texts right back. **Can’t wait. I’ll head over to your place and feed Pancake and Waffles. I picked up our favorites from Wicked Wok.**

My heart melts at the thought of Everett volunteering to feed my sweet cats. And for the record, he’s indulged me with Chinese food nearly every single night since Noah’s accident. Everett is a keeper for sure. Noah is a keeper, too, thus the pickle I’ve landed myself in. Everett and I would have a wonderful life. I bet our kids would all have his cobalt blue eyes. Noah would be a great father for sure. Not to mention our sweet little kidlettes would probably get his bright green eyes and dimples. Yes, Noah would make a great father.

I stop short.

A father! Oh my word. I forgot all about that test.

Lainey comes back, waving something at me. It looks like a small white vial.

"What is that?" For a moment my heart thumps wildly thinking she found the test I was hiding in her bathroom, but it's a clear glass test tube of some kind filled with pink sand.

"It's for you. A woman at the library is all into warding off evil spirits, so I told her about your bad luck and she brought this in today. It's a vial of salt from the Baltic Sea. She says you have to sleep with it under your pillow to scare off all the dead bodies you keep magnetizing to."

"Lainey," I say her name curt enough for her to realize I'm not buying it. "First, you can't scare off a dead body. It simply doesn't work that way. Second, I suggest you take this and put it in your spice rack to help ward off all that bad luck you've been having in the kitchen. You are in charge of baking the pies for the Donovan family Thanksgiving, remember?" I tease as I dash off to the restroom again.

"You're not funny."

"I get that from you," I shout back.

No sooner do I lock the door to the bathroom than I pull out that stick from behind the pumpkin and freeze.

There it is. A giant plus sign stares back at me with the word *pregnant* printed right beneath it, plain as day.

"Holy stars above Honey Hollow."

I'm having Noah's baby.

6

Several days whiz by in a blur, and I find myself bumbling through life.

Noah has yet to make an appearance since the night of the murder.

Everett, thankfully, has been a prince, taking me to the hospital each night to visit with Noah, holding me tight, whispering that Noah will be just fine, that he could feel it in his bones. And strangely enough, I do believe Everett right down to his very wise bones. Everett dabbles in the truth for a living. Somehow, I think I'm at the bottom of the list of people he'd lie to. And that's exactly why I've decided that I can't lie to him either. At the end of this day, I'm going to let him in on my little maternal secret.

The Cutie Pie Bakery and Cakery is filling up with an unusually high volume of women of a certain demographic this afternoon.

"Lily," I whisper. "What's happening?" Honestly, I haven't slept two winks in three days, and I'm far too exhausted to put this or any other mystery to bed.

Geez—the killer! Trisha's killer is still out there somewhere, and if I don't get on the scent quickly, I'm liable to lose this one. I haven't let a killer get away yet. And, personally, I don't want to ruin my streak.

"It's the naughty book club." She shakes her head. "Keelie asked yesterday if it was all right to host it here and you said, 'yeah, sure.'"

My fingers fly to my lips. "I don't remember that." My goodness, what else don't I remember? That pregnancy brain fog I read about must be real, and it must be hitting me hard already.

As soon as I left Lainey's house, I came home and cuddled up with Pancake and Waffles and googled any and everything I could find out about this condition Noah gifted me—and, he had better not have given it to me as a parting gift.

Noah had better fight with everything he's got to pull through. As much as I'd love to start a family, the thought of going it alone absolutely terrifies me.

And my goodness, *Noah*. What am I going to say? Am I really going to confess to him in his disembodied state that he's about to become a father? If Cormack's driving didn't kill him, then this might just finish him off. He'll feel terrible if he doesn't survive. Instead of enjoying paradise, he'll be tormented forever.

No, I can't tell Noah. Not yet anyway. I need to get my head about me.

"Lottie?" Keelie shakes me by the shoulders, and I'm startled to see her standing before me. "Lottie Lemon, is anyone home?" She waves a hand before my face, and I blink back to life.

Lily is already serving up coffee to the masses, and the entire café is overrun with Naomi's naughty book club. All of the usual cohorts are here, and I spot both Mom and Carlotta seated in the corner. Mom has her laptop out and an entire mess of legal pads surrounding her while Carlotta is fully facing Naomi's coital crew.

"Lottie, can I get you some coffee?" Keelie fans me with her apron.

"Coffee? No, no coffee." Coffee is a no-no for those in a delicate condition such as mine, and my decaf has a reputation for giving even the most sensitive to caffeine the jitters. I'm not risking it. Nothing can happen to Noah's baby—my baby, *our* baby.

My hand rises instinctively to my stomach and Keelie glances down.

"Do you have a stomachache?"

"No." I gasp because the alternatives are slim. "I mean, yes. Everett brought home a bag from the Wicked Wok again. I think the Kung Pao chicken was a bit too spicy."

She flexes a wry smile. "Don't worry, Lot. I'll help Lily with the book club. You just go sit out there and enjoy. We still have a few minutes. Why don't you take a break and eat something? I hear the pumpkin pie is to die for." She gives a little wink before taking off to help the masses that are eager to break down the salacious contents of the book at hand.

The bell chimes and an entire army of women in yoga pants and ponytails wander on in.

Lily speeds over and groans, "Worlds are colliding, Lottie. Can we fit the Swift Cycle class *and* the naughty book club in here all at once?"

"I think we're about to find out."

I help Lily fill all the orders, and sure enough once the sweaty Bettys figure out what Naomi's naughty girls are up to, they take note—and they take a seat. It looks as if Naomi just expanded her literary reach in a sweaty single bound.

Finally, both Britney and Cormack file in still wearing their spandex finery, both with their hair up in the requisite ponytail.

Both women are blondes and both women once had intimate relations with Noah.

"Lila." Britney's cherry red lips flicker in lieu of a smile.

"Louella." Cormack offers a somber nod.

And neither one of them has the ability to say my name. I'm not sure why, but this little alphabet jumble has been going on for quite a while now.

"You're just in time. The fun is about to start." I hitch my head over to the brimming crowd taking over the café. "What can I get you, ladies?"

"A pumpkin spice latte for me," Britney says it curt as if she found the drink offensive on some level. She turns and glowers at Naomi.

"I'll take the same." Cormack wiggles as if she's got something cooking she can hardly wait to share.

"What is it?" I flatline. Face it, I'm not all that interested, but at the moment, it can take my mind off the fact the father of my child, my legal husband, is being kept alive by modern technology.

Cormack's celadon eyes widen. "I've got a hot date this afternoon."

Britney and I exchange a brief glance.

"A lunch date?" I muse. And considering Noah hasn't eaten lunch in nearly two weeks, it looks as if he's finally off her radar.

Cormack grimaces. "A dinner date, actually. We're hitting the early bird special at the Evergreen."

Britney bubbles with a laugh. "Running with the geriatric crowd these days, Featherby?"

"Yes, she is." I take the liberty of answering for her. "You're going to dinner with Topper Blakley, aren't you?"

Her mouth falls open and she quickly seeks out my mother while attempting to hush me.

"Would you keep it down, Lynn?"

"Cormack, that's my mother's twisted gentleman caller you're flirting with. Although, we both know you're doing more than flirting. Everett and I spotted the two of you in the woods that night." Okay, so it was Noah and me, but I'm not going anywhere near that truth.

Cormack takes a breath and doesn't dare let it go.

"That's right," I snip. "I caught you with your hand in the *nookie* jar. And with that old goat? Really?" I'm about to tell her she can do better when a dangerously delicious thought comes to mind. "Keep up the good work."

Both she and Britney blink back in disbelief.

"I mean it," I say. "The two of you are a far better fit than my mother and he will ever be. You're upper crust and my mother is middle earth. She's not even in the same tax bracket. It would never work. But you and Topper"—a husky laugh growls from me—"you click like fine wine. Face it, the two of you come from the same extravagant world. You above anyone else will understand how to spend his billions on quality luxury items." I lean in as if I'm about to spill some serious juicy morsels. "My mother still shops secondhand."

Cormack straightens. "I'm so sorry to hear that. And to be frank, Topper would find that intolerable. I'm afraid for both their sakes I'll have to step in. Now, if you'll excuse me." She pulls a copy of that book everyone is toting. "I just finished this steamy gem last night." She flashes the cover my way.

"*Her Baby's Daddy*." I jump a little as I read it. My entire body feels as if it's experienced a mild jolt of electrocution.

Cormack moans as she looks to the morbidly pregnant woman on the cover while a man with long hair and a tan chest attempts to catch her as she faints.

I'm about to faint. It's as if the universe knew this embryonic fate would befall me and chose this book and its perverted procreative methods to taunt me.

Cormack scuttles off and Britney leans in.

"Why in the world would you give her the okay to steal your mama's man?"

"Because my mama's man is a nutcase who runs a dating app for swingers, for starters. And secondly, he's already cheated on her with Cormack. I say she can have him. And if she's tangled up with someone else, then that means I get Noah all to myself."

She comes shy of grimacing. "Lena, you do realize he's not doing well."

"Yes, but Noah is a fighter. He's going to pull through." My hand comes inches within cupping my belly again. "He has to."

She gives a single nod before darting her eyes over to Naomi. "You're good at solving murders, aren't you, Libby?"

"So they say. Why?" The proof is in the homicidal pudding, but I'm not one to boast of my crime-busting accomplishments.

"Because you might just stumble upon another body soon. I'm feeling a bit homicidal myself."

"*Ooh*. Who are you going to kill?"

"Naomi Sawyer." She stalks off and takes a seat just as the steamy meeting gets underway.

Naomi? Now that's a crime spree I want the details on sooner than later, but judging by the fact the naughty meeting is about to get underway, I opt for later for now.

I'm about to walk over and fill that empty seat between my mother and Carlotta just as my half-sisters, Kelleth and Aspen, run in with a rather familiar looking young woman and head straight for the café. Both Kelleth and Aspen have vanilla blonde hair. Kelleth is tall and waiflike, and Aspen looks like a blonde Betty Boop. But that girl with them, there's something about her that resonates and I can't quite put my finger on why. Her short copper hair is curled under her jawline, her skin glows bronze, and just as she whips out her own copy of *Her Baby's Daddy*, I realize where I've seen her before.

It's her! The young woman who whispered something to Trisha the night she was murdered and had her turning white as a ghost before she ever became one.

Aspen scoots in close to her and they begin to whisper and giggle.

Would you look at that? She's friends with my sisters. It looks as if investigating my first suspect just became a little easier.

I'm about to head that way when a tall, dark, and handsome figure walks right through the door, and I do mean through it—glass and all, followed by a gloriously gorgeous llama.

"Noah," I whisper with all the excitement I can muster and he presses out a dimpled grin my way.

He holds his hand out and I covertly take it.

"Let's get to the kitchen," he whispers as if someone might hear him and it only endears me to him all the more.

Gemma, that giant giddy llama, clip-clops forward, looking ever so adorable with her blonde curly mane and those impossibly long lashes.

"We've got a suspect in our midst, don't we, Lottie?" Her voice warbles as if she were about to break into song.

I nod and point to the crowd in general just as Naomi begins reading aloud a particularly steamy passage, that if I'm not mistaken leads to the aforementioned baby.

"Oh dear"—Gemma clacks her way over—"I've never heard a riveting tale like this before."

"Poor Gemma," I whisper and I usher Noah off into my rather microscopic office—think airline toilet—and seal the door shut behind us.

I wrap my arms around him tight and pull back to look at this magnificent man.

"I love you so much." My entire body quivers as I say it.

"I love you, too, Lottie." He brushes a kiss over my lips, and as magical as it is, I can hardly feel it this time.

"You've been gone," I say. "Where were you?"

"I'm sorry. I really don't have any control over this at all. I was in my body. I think I heard you and Everett last night. You were whispering in my ear, and I tried my hardest to grasp every word."

"Oh, Noah, that's a good sign, right?"

His brows pinch in the middle. "Yes, but this?" He glances down at this glowing blue frame. "This is sort of a bad sign."

My lungs seize, and I can't catch my next breath. "You mean, when you're here with me, you're—"

He gives a simple nod. "On the verge of death."

I do my best to swat him, but my hand keeps falling right through his body. "Get back there, Noah. I'd much rather have you fighting the good fight than making out with me in the office."

His chest bounces with a laugh. "Again, I only have so much control. Besides"—his expression sobers up—"I don't think we should, you know, get physical in this state. It's not right. It's not fair to you, psychologically speaking."

"To heck with my sanity. I'm okay with physical."

Noah closes his eyes a moment before dotting my lips with a kiss. "That's about as comfortable as I am taking it. If anything happens to me"—he swallows hard as if he had to—"I want you to know that I'm rooting for you and Everett."

My heart crumbles to dust just like that, and more than anything I want to tell him about our baby.

Just as I open my mouth and struggle to get the words out, there's a knock on the other side of the door.

Noah's entire being lights up in a spray of swirling light as he dissipates to nothing right before my eyes. It's a thing of beauty. And it's the saddest thing I've ever seen. As much as I want him back in his body fighting for his life, a very greedy part of me wants him here with me.

The knocking persists and I open the door to find Judge Essex Everett Baxter standing on the other side looking like a handsome devil with just the right amount of stubble peppering his cheeks.

"Lemon? Are you all right?" There's a marked level of concern in his voice that I haven't heard before.

"I'm fine." I clear my throat. "Noah was here for just a moment. I guess he got sucked back into his body."

"As strange as it sounds, I'm hoping it's a good thing. Do you think you can come on a little drive with me? I have something to show you."

"Sure. As soon as I talk to suspect number one," I say, taking his hand and leading him to the register.

The pretty girl next to Aspen blows my sisters a kiss before cinching her purse and slinking to the door. She turns a moment and her eyes hook to Everett. Her lips part and you can see her hormonal alarm going off at the sight of him. You can't really blame the girl. Everett is a showstopper.

She licks her lips in anticipation before heading out under the cover of a stormy sky.

And just like that, I lose my opportunity to kick this case into gear.

7

Everett says not to worry about where we're going because where we're going is a surprise.

That's one of the many things that I love about Everett, the fact that he never fails to surprise me in the very best way—with his enthusiastic kisses, the way he makes breakfast in the morning, the way he's prone to blanketing the inside of my house with flowers on occasion, the way he's always willing to go on an adventure with me at a moment's notice, the way he loves me with such zest and fervor. There are billions of women who would die happy to have Everett love them that way just for a day—and here he's offered his heart to me in that manner for a lifetime.

But, as of late, I'm full of surprises, too—a very tiny surprise that is currently busy knitting itself together in my womb.

I fully plan on telling him about Noah Junior brewing in my belly. I've spent my entire life in a fit of independence, and don't get me wrong, I don't plan on changing that any time soon, but Everett is the one person I trust with my deepest, darkest secret. More than anything I'd like to share this with him.

We drive along the highway and I soak in the hillsides covered with fall leaves of every color, fiery reds, pale gold, deep burgundy, and persimmon. We pass the orchard with its colorful apples that hang like Christmas tree ornaments. We pass the pumpkin patch that glows in peachy hues, their cheery globes dotting the ground with an abundance of color. Finally, we exit at Hollyhock, a small quaint town just to the east of Honey Hollow, and it just so happens to be the town that Noah grew up in until his father moved them to Fallbrook to live with Everett's family. It's hard for me to believe that these two fantastic men were always within driving distance of my life at any given time. What I wouldn't give to have known them far sooner than we met. I wonder how our lives would be different if we knew each other in our formative years. But I suppose things happen for a reason. And, as it stands, I met both Noah and Everett on the same fateful day just over a year ago.

Everett takes a left into the hillside, and as the elevation changes, the maples, the sweetgums, the oaks, and ambers all cluster together and put on a spectacular show of autumn splendor. A creek runs along our left and there are evergreens that line our path all the way up to a large wooden arch with a sign that reads *Maple Meadows Lodge.*

A mammoth wooden building—an overgrown cabin that looks just as beautiful as any chalet with its Lincoln log design stained a dark brown with pine green trim around the windows—sits up ahead with an enormous parking lot that's currently sparsely populated. It looks more or less like your run-of-the-mill lodge that my family used to stay at when we would drive up for ski trips. There's a ski lift a few miles away and I can see a small lake on the north side of the property.

Everett and I hop out and take in the fresh mountain air perfumed with evergreens and the earthy soil below our feet.

"We're here." Everett pulls me in close as we look up at the monolithic structure.

"Do they have a restaurant?" I'm a bit puzzled as to why we're here.

His chest thumps with a dry laugh. "I don't think we're that lucky, Lemon."

"Are we renting a room for the afternoon?" Heaven knows I could use some shut-eye, and an afternoon nap wrapped in Everett's arms sounds perfectly blissful.

"We could get lucky if you want, Lemon."

"*Everett*. What is it then?"

He takes a breath. "Hook Redwood called and let me know this was the place Noah was trying to negotiate the offer on."

A horrible groan comes from me. "That's right. Noah was looking to buy a lodge up in Hollyhock. Oh my goodness, this is it." I take a look around and see it with new eyes. "Oh, Everett, he wanted to invest in this place for the future of his family. He wanted to have something substantial to offer his children one day. My heart breaks just being here." And the fact I have one of his children tucked in my body makes me ache for Noah and his precious dreams all the more.

Everett drops a heated kiss over my forehead. "Let's take a tour."

We walk around the property, which boasts of fishing in the summer, snow play in the winter, an archery range, and the potential for a corral. We step into the grand entry, and there's a two-story river rock fireplace against the south wall with a roaring fire glowing and crackling as guests sit around it reading and sipping hot beverages.

There's a stone reception area with a couple of staff members in uniform and they offer us a cheery greeting. Everett lets them know we're here to check out the property as a potential investment, and the grounds manager is quick to show us the cozy dining hall with its oversized antler chandelier, the kitchen with its old but sturdy professional grade appliances, and a few of the nicer rooms with views of the lake.

Everything is simply adorable, and everything is simply in need of some slight renovation.

Finally, Everett and I head to the lake and take a seat on a boulder as we face the adorable lodge.

"Fifty-five rooms," Everett says as he exhales hard. "Hook says it has a booking rate of about eighty percent year-round. He said it would be profitable, day one. Noah was going to put down half in cash and take a loan on the rest, hoping it would pay itself off."

"This is no small purchase. Fifty-five rooms plus a staff and a maintenance schedule that I'm assuming is pretty rigorous. What do they want for this place?"

Everett pulls out his phone and shows me the email Hook sent him.

"Oh my goodness. Is that in American dollars?" I about have a heart attack looking at all those zeros attached at the end. And, my word, Noah has enough to put down half? No wonder Cormack was determined to sink her hooks into him. Noah could afford more designer bags than I gave him credit for. I know his dad left him and his brother a lot of money. Noah is the one who paid for my kitchen at the bakery, after all. I guess he had a nice chunk of change left over.

Everett's chest rumbles once again. "Real estate isn't cheap around here. Hollyhock is nice. People love it. I think there's a lot of untapped potential with this place, and Noah saw it."

"Noah," I whisper his name like a secret. "Everett, I inherited an awful lot of land and properties through Nell.

I'll sell one, trade it, anything. I just have to buy this place for Noah."

For our child, but I leave that little genetic detail out of the conversation for now. Once I get that verbal ball rolling, it won't stop for eighteen years and beyond. Suddenly, the responsibility of having a child feels daunting.

Who will watch the bakery?

Who will watch my precious child?

Will it have Noah's emerald green eyes and dimples? Goodness, I hope so.

Tears come and I can't seem to fight them.

"Hey?" Everett pulls me in and wraps his arms around me tight, warming me from the icy autumn breeze. "You're shivering. Come on. Let's get out of here, and I'll take you to lunch."

I nod as I look to the beautiful lodge one more time. "Take me straight to Redwood Reality. I want this property, Everett. I have to buy it for Noah."

"Lemon, if you buy it, this place will be yours." He pulls back and bears those lake blue eyes into mine. "Noah, he might not—"

"I know." I glance to the ground, afraid of that very outcome. My hand glides to my tummy. "It doesn't matter, Everett. I need this lodge. This is already mine. I can feel it."

"Okay then." He takes a deep breath as he looks around. "I'll let Hook know we're interested."

And we do. We put in a call to Hook, and he's thrilled to hear we're saving the day for Noah.

"What's the down payment?" I ask. "How soon can I sign the papers and close the deal?"

Hook laughs from the other end of the line. "I'm glad you're excited, Lottie. They're asking for a ten thousand dollar deposit. I can start up the paperwork and send it to you to sign electronically."

"Yes, please." I poke Everett on the arm. "Just ten thousand dollars? This is easier than I thought."

Hook groans, "That's just to secure the property while you get your loan together. You can put down as much as you like. Obviously, the more you put down, the less you'll owe."

"I see." I'm not a numbers person by far, but with all the real estate Nell gave me, I should quickly become one. "What's the minimum down?"

Hook breathes into the phone. "The minimum would be a couple hundred thousand. But if you did that, your mortgage on the place would be pretty steep. You might get yourself in over your head that way."

"A couple hundred thousand?" I say, stunned. "I'm already in over my head. Hook, I don't have that."

"I do," Everett says into the phone. I'll talk to my loan guy and see what we can swing. Get the paperwork going and consider it sold."

We hang up with Hook, and I look up at Everett in awe. "Everett, I'll pay you back—every dime."

"No, Lemon. Noah will pay me back." The tips of his lips curl upward. "And if he's unable to do that—" He sighs as he examines the lodge as the wind swirls around us, blowing the colorful fall foliage right out of the trees and sending it into the sky like confetti. "It looks as if you and I are about to become brand new owners of the Maple Meadows Lodge."

"Everett!" I wrap my arms around him and plant a wet one right over his lips. "You don't know how happy this makes me." Tears glitter in my eyes and my adrenaline kicks up a notch because I can feel the words bubbling up in my throat. I pull back and plant my hands firmly over his chest. "I have something to tell you, Everett. And here at Maple Meadows with the deep blue lake behind us, the woods, fall in all its splendor—I couldn't think of a better place to do it."

His arms float around my waist, his expression firmly sober.

"What is it, Lemon? You can tell me anything. I won't judge you. If you need my help, I won't ask questions."

I give a little shrug. "Not even if I have a body to hide?"

A dull chuckle bounces through him. "Especially not then. Of course, I'd help you hide it."

"You would do that for me?" Every last bit of me melts at the prospect.

"You bet I would." His cobalt eyes rake over my features, hot as coals. I have always been able to feel

Everett's gaze as he examines me as sure as a touch. That's a part of his magic.

"I'm glad you're not going to pass any judgments—even though it's technically demanded of you on a daily basis." My heart pounds over my chest, drumming into my throat and out my ears. As soon as I say it, this baby becomes real in a whole new way. It's as if I'm about to unleash it into the world, and here it's still at home in the safety of my body.

"Everett—" His name comes out in a ragged whisper, and I can hardly catch my breath. "I just want you to know I wasn't expecting this. It was completely unplanned."

"What is it, Lemon?" His features fill with concern. And if I'm not mistaken, he looks frightened for me. "What's got you rattled?"

I press my gaze hard into his stormy blue eyes. His strong arms hold me and comfort me.

"Everett, I'm pregnant. I'm having Noah's baby."

8

"A baby."

Everett hasn't stopped repeating those words ever since we got back from Hollyhock. As soon as I spilled my secret, Everett stood there stunned for a few seconds before he twirled me around and kissed me over the mouth until I was dizzy. He then promptly informed me I would make the best mother in the world. And Everett has been beaming with pride ever since. It's late in the afternoon and the sun is ready to vacate our end of the world.

He drove me straight home and landed me on the couch with a blanket and enough pillows nestled around me to furnish that fifty-five room beast, the Maple Meadows Lodge, we just decided to purchase. Of all the places I could have told him the precious news, I'm glad it was right there, at the lodge where Noah decided to purchase something for his family. It only seems right.

Everett gets a fire going and brings me hot chamomile tea. He takes off my shoes and gently rubs my feet as if it were his job.

"We need to know everything there is about having a baby, Lemon." He pulls his phone out and begins googling away. "There's no time to waste."

"I'm pretty sure we have nine months."

"It sounds like we've lost time already."

We. I swoon at the thought. How every part of me dissolves with relief that Everett wants to be a part of this process. Even if Noah were right here with us, I wouldn't want it any other way.

Pancake and Waffles hop up and land on my lap. They're just as soft as any of these pillows propping me up.

"Whoa," Everett says as he carefully pulls Waffles onto his own lap, and I move Pancake over a notch. "I'll look up pregnancy and cats and see what they say."

"Oh, I'm not allergic, that's for sure. And I don't think I can get an allergy just because I'm having a baby."

He shakes his head as he stares into his phone. "It says here kitty litter could be dangerous. I don't think you can keep the cats."

"There's no way I'm getting rid of my family," I say, amused as I take a sip of the chamomile tea he's whipped up for me.

"We can keep them at my place."

"They'll be lonely because you'll be here." I bite down playfully over my bottom lip as I say it.

"You bet I will. And truth be told, I'm not sorry one bit I'm extending my stay."

A giggle bounces through me. "Truth be told, Everett, I enjoy having you here every minute with me. You really have brought me so much comfort—you know, with almost losing Noah. Country Cottage Road doesn't feel the same without him. Every time I see the lights on at night across the street, for a brief moment I forget that Britney is staying there with Toby and I get a glimmer of hope that I might see Noah."

Everett pulls my feet up over his lap and begins rubbing them once again and it feels like heaven.

He pumps an all too brief smile. "I'll take care of the kitty litter. I don't want you anywhere near it. It's not safe for you right now. I've already ordered up to a half of dozen books on what to expect while you're expecting. They should be here by tomorrow. We'll need a doctor. A good one. If you don't have one, I'll ask around. We're only shooting for the best. And, of course, I'll accompany you to all of your appointments. That is, if you want me to."

"Are you insane? Yes, I would love for you to. But I'd hate for you to miss work."

"Don't worry about the courthouse. We'll work the courthouse around this baby."

"Everett." I pull his hand forward and kiss it. "Okay, I'll make sure the doctor's appointments work with your schedule. We could go to the Wicked Wok after the appointments and have lunch. That sounds like fun."

"It's a standing date." He tips his head, examining me. "Do you want me to call in for some Wicked Wok right now? Are you having a craving?"

A laugh bounces through me. "I'm fine. Go ahead and turn on the TV. We'll watch a game if you want. I need to text Aspen about something anyway."

"Sounds good to me." He grabs the remote, and the television above the fireplace flickers to life. "Whatever you need from me, money, time, advice, the sky's the limit, Lemon. Everything I have, everything I am is yours."

"Everett"—I say, breathless—"your love is all I'll ever need."

He gets right back to rubbing my feet, and I get right to texting Aspen.

Hello, Aspen, this is me, Lottie. Who was your friend that came by the bakery with you this morning? The pretty girl with the copper hair? She looked familiar and I couldn't place her. I hit send and suddenly realize I should probably back this up with a good reason to pester her. **I think she left her sweater at the shop.** I hit send again. There. Nothing like a little white lie to save the day. Of course, I remember the girl from the night of the murder. Her name was Annette, I think. Anyway, I'm dying to pump as much information from my sister as I possibly can. At least this way the wheels of the investigation are still spinning.

Aspen herself was a quasi-suspect in a murder investigation a few months back and was grateful I didn't handcuff her on the spot when I questioned her. She shook like a leaf when she confessed to being a part of the Elite Entourage, a high priced "dating" service that caters to wealthy and perverse men alike. It's basically a front for a prostitution ring. And as if it wasn't bad enough that one of my half-sisters found gainful employment there, Kelleth began working there as well a few months back.

I keep meaning to threaten them within an inch of their lives to get them to leave the seedy organization, but the right opportunity never seems to present itself. Besides, from what I hear, they don't have to sleep with anyone. The girls control how far they want their so-called dates to go, and according to both of them they leave after dinner. I'm sure they wouldn't confess to the contrary to me anyhow. We're not exactly what I would consider close.

My phone pings and it's a response from Aspen.

Hello, Lottie. (I can practically feel the sarcasm coming off the screen.) **That was Annette Havershem. She's a good friend from work—yes, *that* work. And yes, I realize that she was at the charity event the night of the murder. I also realize that she didn't leave her sweater behind at your bakery since she**

almost did and I made it a point to give it back her. Do you know what else I realize?

Her message cuts off with the cliffhanger.

Great. I slump into the sofa as Pancake looks up at me with a bored look on his face.

What else do you realize, Aspen? I'm sure you're dying to let me know.

My phone pings again.

You're investigating her, just like you investigated me. I get it. And no, I won't say anything. But I will tell you that Nettie had nothing to do with the murder of that woman.

I sniff at the phone, a little indignant that she called me out so boldly. And, fine, she just so happened to humble me all at the same time.

Where can I find Nettie? I hit send and can practically feel her sighing as she inspects my text.

A few minutes drift by, and just when I'm about to doze off with my head against Pancake's body, my phone pings back to life.

There's a mixer tonight in the Onyx Lounge at the Regal Hotel. Most of the EE will be there. I'm pretty sure she won't miss it. There's a huge business convention being held there all week, lots of fertile ground to cover. I suppose we'll see you there.

Ugh. Fertile ground? Any of the girls in the Elite Entourage will be lucky if they don't find themselves in my position. Not that I'm unlucky. Quite frankly, single mother or not, I'm the luckiest girl in the world. My hand floats to my belly as I look over at Everett and my heart swells to the size of the room.

He gives my knee a quick pat. "Don't worry, Lemon. We're doing this together."

"Good, because we have a date in the Onyx Lounge at the Regal Hotel in just a few short hours."

"No way, no how. I smell an investigation afoot and I want you to consider bowing out of this one—and perhaps every one after that."

"No way, no how, Baxter. I'll be at the Onyx room tonight whether you'll be there or not."

Everett purses his lips, his stony blue eyes pressed hard over mine.

"I guess it's a date."

"I guess it is."

And I couldn't be happier.

For whatever reason, my need for justice feels just as necessary as my need to breathe.

Besides, Trisha Maples still needs justice. And I plan on giving it to her.

9

The Regal Hotel in downtown Fallbrook stands erect like a glittering tower with its gold embossed signage. The ten-foot-tall glass doors give way to a sweeping marble entry dripping with rows of crystal chandeliers and a reception counter that looks as if it goes on for miles. There's a black rhinestone sign that reads *Onyx Lounge* to our left and our party moves as one large procession in that direction.

Of course, once I found out the Onyx Lounge was open to any and everyone, I invited Keelie and Bear to tag along. And you have no idea how hard it was not to blurt out my good news to Keelie about the baby—but, seeing that Noah's ghost could be roaming just about anywhere at any given time, I'm afraid he might hear the good news from someone other than me. Keelie has never professed to be an expert at keeping secrets.

Both Everett and I agreed that I should consider it carefully before telling Noah about the baby at all. He could either be so thrilled that the news makes him fight harder to live or despondent over the idea that he may not be here to help raise our child—it could do him in quickly. I feel like I'm playing with fire, and I'll do anything to protect Noah from getting burned.

Keelie and Bear quickly arrive with Keelie in a fitted blue dress and Bear looking as if he just stepped off a construction site. Bear has sandy blond shaggy hair and a ruddy complexion from spending his fair share of time outdoors. He owns and operates his own construction company. In fact, he's the one that Nell hired to put together the bakery.

No sooner do we exchange a quick greeting than I note Alex and Lily heading this way.

Lily has her hair down in long, luscious, dark waves and she's poured herself into a little black dress that comes up high on the neck and short around the thighs. I don't see any sign of Naomi, so it looks as if Lily is winning this round in the fight for Alex Fox's heart. Alex looks so much like Noah tonight. My eyes burn with tears at the sight of him.

"Sorry, Lot." Keelie wraps an arm around my shoulders as we watch them head this way. "Lily was there when you threw out the invite."

"I don't mind one bit."

Lily flexes a smile. "Naomi said she'd be here soon. Let's head in. Maybe there's still time to lose her in the crowd."

Keelie, Bear, and Lily speed into the Onyx Lounge, but Alex steps in close to Everett and me as if he were about to say something profound.

My word, what if he knows about the baby? But *how* would he know? It's not like there's a neon sign going off in my belly that's exposing my secret.

And then it hits me.

"Is it Noah?" A horrible feeling grips my chest. "We can leave right now and be at Honey Hollow General in twenty minutes. Twenty minutes. That's enough time for the world to change."

"Noah is fine. In fact, I just left the hospital." Alex flexes those dimples and my heart breaks for his brother all over again. What I wouldn't do to get those dimples of Noah's to dig in one more time for me. "I just wanted to let the two of you know I finally tracked down my mother. She was in Hawaii at some technology-free resort. But she's home now in Florida and come tomorrow she'll be on the first flight to Vermont. I'm picking her up in Burlington."

A breath gets caught in my throat. "Your mom?" I forgot all about the fact he's been trying to reach her. Tears moisten my eyes once again. Noah has only ever spoken briefly of his mother. All I know is that she lives in Florida. I don't even know why Noah and Alex ended up moving from one bad marriage to the next with their swindler of a father. Noah's father has long since passed away, and that's about all I know regarding his family history.

"That's great," Everett says, picking up my hand and it feels so natural this way with him. "I look forward to seeing Suze again."

"Suze? Short for Suzanna?" I inquire, completely thrilled at the prospect of meeting the woman who is basically my mother-in-law *and* the grandmother to my child.

Alex cinches his lips. "Yes, but if you call her that, she'll shoot on sight. It's just Suze. Don't get your hopes up for any warm and fuzzy meeting. Our mother is a special brand of woman. She's maternal to a point."

Everett nods as if acknowledging this. "And she's likable to a point."

They share a brief chuckle on her behalf, and now I'm worried about whether or not Suze will find *me* likable to a point. I want her to like me. Heck, I want her to love me.

We head into the club and are immediately engulfed with the thumping of thrashing loud music. It's wall-to-wall bodies in here as if the entire adult population of the hotel had drained into this orifice. The floor is glossy and black, there are tables set out everywhere along with round white sofas, and every spare seat is filled. The bar is lined with people all clamoring for a drink, and I can't help but notice how glamorous all the women look, so young and beautiful.

The men are all dressed in suits, looking every bit as dapper as Everett, albeit they're nowhere near his league.

The scent of alcohol mingling with expensive perfume fills our senses and my nose twitches as if it's had its fill of both.

Lily scuttles back over to Alex and hooks her arm through his. "This place is crawling with hookers! Lottie, attach yourself to Everett lest one of these floozies tries to steal your man."

I do as I'm told, and I do it quickly. Everett belongs to me. I've licked him in more places than one. He's definitely mine.

I lean toward Lily. "How can you tell these women are hookers? They look gorgeous, young, and healthy. They could be anybody." Like my half-sisters, but I leave Kelleth and Aspen out of it for now. Naomi, too. She's worked for the EE before. A fact that I'm willing to bet she doesn't plan on showing off to Alex.

Lily scoffs. "One of my old sorority sisters is a higher-up in the organization. She's here, of course, and she tipped me off that every girl with one of those thick rose gold bangles on her wrist belongs to them. It's like a calling card so the men looking for a good time will be able to identify who to flock to."

I glance around, and sure enough there's a thick rose gold bracelet on just about every girl here.

"I suppose if you didn't belong to the EE and you happened to stumble into club Onyx, it would be a bad time to wear a rose gold bracelet tonight," I say.

Lily nods. "You'd better tell your new sisters. I saw both Kelleth and Aspen in the back wearing that exact same hardware on their wrists." She tugs at Alex. "Come on. Let's dance. Then I'll let you ply me with drinks and take me to your place."

"Not so fast," a female voice calls from behind and we turn to find Naomi standing tall in a stunning pink number that clings to her skin—and an all too familiar face by her side, my half-brother.

"Finn!" I say as I leap over and offer him a firm embrace. Finn and I get along a heck of a lot better than I do with my new sisters. He's down-to-earth and sweet and funny—and dating Britney, not Naomi. And then it hits me why Britney threatened to murder Naomi earlier today. "You're not cheating on Britney with Naomi, are you?"

Finn stiffens. Finn has that handsome, wholesome boy next-door appeal, with caramel wavy hair and dark eyes. He's the manager up at the Sugar Bowl Resort, but seems to be spending most of his time in Honey Hollow as of late—or Fallbrook as it were.

"No, I'm not," he says as Naomi and Lily begin to squabble. "Naomi said she wanted to talk about coordinating clients and events between the Evergreen and the Sugar Bowl, but I'm beginning to feel I was ambushed. Brit is going to kill me. She's been telling me all along that Naomi was after me."

"It looks like she's right," Everett says.

I wince over at Alex, who's currently trying to break up the hostilities between the two ex-friends.

"Actually, she might be wrong," I say. "I think Naomi is using you to try to make Alex jealous."

Finn closes his eyes a moment. "Great. I've always wanted to be used to help someone out with another relationship." His chest bounces with the prospect. "You know what, I'll do it. One and done. But she just gets tonight. In fact, I'll text Brit and let her know I'm helping out a friend. And when I see her later, I'll let her know exactly what happened."

Everett takes a breath. "Good luck with that. I've met Brit. She could take you. Venture carefully."

Everett moves us deeper into the club, and we weave and bob our way through partially clad bodies, each one more beautiful than the last, until I spot a cluster of familiar faces near the back right where Lily said they would be.

"Look at that, Everett." I casually nod to the rear of the room. "My sisters are there and so is Annette." The copper-haired beauty stands tall in a silver dress that looks ten sizes too small. It scoops low in the front and hardly covers the top of her thighs.

She glances this way and immediately her eyes hook to Everett. I can't help but make a face at the sight. Sure, I get it. Everett is hard to resist, but something about the way her face brightens every time she sees him doesn't sit well with me.

"Maybe you should go over and talk to her?" I frown as I say it. "As much as I hate the thought of her thinking that you want to take her to your room, I think she'd sell you the moon just as quick as she'd sell you her body."

Everett presses those gorgeous eyes to mine. "I'll head over and see what she has to say about that night and about Trisha. Just remember this. I love you, Lemon—and I love that baby. There's not a woman in the world who has the power to lure me to her room but you." He gives my hand a squeeze before ditching into the crowd, and I swoon hard at the way Everett Baxter loves me.

I'm about to head over to my sisters when a brilliant shock of light erupts over the dance floor, and soon I'm being swayed to the rhythm of the music by a dashing ghost—the exact ghost who just so happened to have knocked me up.

"Noah!" I wrap my arms around him and he feels incredibly solid. I pull his cheeks forward and land a long, smothering kiss over his lips and I don't care how insane I happen to look.

"Whoa." A laugh gets caught in his throat. His dark hair is slicked back, and he's dressed in a suit, blending in impeccably with the men in this room. "I'm glad you're happy to see me, Lot." He looks around. "Where did Gemma go? We arrived at the very same time."

"I'm here," the warbling voice of a female trills from behind and I look to find my favorite llama swaying from side to side as if trying to keep up with the funky beat pumping from the speakers. "Goodness, Lottie, you've put on your dancing shoes. And Noah, you do look mighty handsome. Is there a suspect in the vicinity?" She cranes her incredibly long neck as she peruses the dance floor.

"Over there in the back with Everett." I quickly orient them to where he is and spot Annette giggling up at him, flipping her hair, and batting her lashes. "She works for the Elite Entourage. They're hosting a function tonight, so I thought this would be a great time to catch up with her." I sway to the music in the event anyone sees me, they might just think I'm singing along.

Gemma brays out a laugh. "Hey? I can really get into this!" She trots in front of us, her long neck swaying to the rhythm of the music as her feet enjoy an odd little tap dance. "I'll head over and listen in, Lottie. Don't you worry. We'll find Trisha's killer together. They won't get away with this!" Her voice begins to grow faint as she moves through the crowd. "They won't get away with murder!"

"I should hope not."

Noah sighs as he wraps an arm around me, our gaze still set in their direction. "Ivy and I were getting close to doing a complete shutdown of this twisted organization. And here they are, out in full force."

"See? The world needs you, Noah. You have to come back to us." My hand flits to my belly as if it were trying to clue him in on what I have cooking in there.

"I'm trying, Lot. I'm trying my hardest. It's always good to hear your voice. As much as I don't want you camping out at the hospital, it is a treat to hear you. Alex dropped by a little while ago."

"Did he tell you your mother is coming out tomorrow? I can't wait to meet her."

His eyes grow large. "Lottie, I don't recommend you meet my mother."

"What? Don't be silly. Of course, I'm going to meet her. I'm dying to meet her. She's your mother and my mother-in-law. I'm going to love her."

He shakes his head. "No, you won't."

I swat him on the arm as we share a quiet laugh.

"I will. And I'm hoping she'll love me, too."

He winces. "Okay, but don't set your hopes up for something you might not get. And don't say I didn't warn you." He ticks his head to the back again. "So how are you and Everett?"

"We're fine. And we're just friends. We're keeping it chaste. I'm still your wife, Noah. Come back to me, and we'll get right back to where we were."

He sighs as he wraps his arms low around my waist while those sad evergreen eyes bear hard into mine.

"Lottie"—he presses it out with grief—"don't let me drive a wedge between you and Everett. You do what you need to do. I just need to know that you're happy. You should forget about me, Lottie."

My heart breaks hearing him speak those words. He's acquiescing to his dismal physical state and I hate it.

"Noah, I miss you far too much to ever forget about you."

A couple bumps into us from behind and we turn to find a familiar blonde bopping alongside a silver-haired wily fox who is in the process of breaking my mother's heart.

"Cormack. *Topper*," I say, glaring hard at him.

He squints over at me. "Hey ho! What do you know? Are you up for a party with two lovely singles ready to mingle?"

I suck in a quick breath. "You don't even recognize me! My mother is Miranda Lemon in the event you've forgotten her as well. She actually thinks the two of you are dating. Please give her the common courtesy of letting her know what a jackhole you are before traipsing about looking for a threesome!"

"Um buh duh—" his mouth hangs open as he inspects me. "Ah, yes, the baker." It comes out with far less enthusiasm. "Cormie, why don't I get us a drink?" He takes off, and no sooner does he belly up to the bar than he's flanked by a couple of rose gold wearing bracelets.

Noah grunts, " Cormack is really seeing this guy, huh?"

"Don't let your ego take a hit," I'm quick to tell him.

Cormack postures herself while taking pouting to a whole new level. "Thanks, Linda. But look at those girls crawling all over him. Topper is such a catch. It'll be a miracle if I can hold onto a man like that."

I'd ask whatever happened to Noah, but Noah happens to be front and center and I'd hate for him to hear it.

"If only my Noah were here." Her entire body sags and that emerald green strapless gown she's donned looks as if it's about to slip right off her body.

Noah gives his lapels a tug with pride.

"Easy, big boy, you belong to me."

Cormack clicks her tongue. "Noah belongs to me, Lisa. And if you think for one minute I'm trading up because I want to, I have news for you. Noah would want me to take care of myself and be happy. And only someone with Topper Blakley's bank account could even get close to doing that. If I can't have love with Noah, at least I can have a yacht and sixteen homes in twelve different states with Topper. If you'll excuse me, I've got a wallet to secure." She stalks off and expertly shoos those Elite Entourage girls to the wayside.

"She's right, Lottie. I want both of you to be happy. For Cormack, that means diving into the deepest pockets she can find—and for you, that means Everett." Noah lands a soul-melting kiss over my lips. And if he hadn't sealed his mouth over mine, I would have told him all about the precious child we're about to bring into the world. He pulls away slowly and his body begins to shine ever so brightly.

"Noah, wait. There's something I have to tell you!" But it's too late. Noah just zipped right back to his body.

Keelie dances her way over with a fruity drink in hand as Bear does his best to keep up.

"Lottie, are you sure you want that girl crawling all over your man?"

I glance over to find Everett literally attempting to pluck Annette Havershem off his person.

"It doesn't look as if this is going as planned. I'd better intervene. Do you mind if I borrow this?" I say, taking the drink from her.

"Not at all, Lottie."

I fly across the room as if I were the poltergeist in question and pretend to trip just as I come up on the skanky snake trying to climb Mount Baxter. I make sure to spill just enough of the icy drink in my hand over the front of her dress and she hops away from him a good three feet and screams.

"Oh my goodness, I'm so sorry," I shout, but it comes out wooden because I'm not sorry in the least.

Gemma appears before us, jumping and braying out a laugh. "Good one, Lottie! I was afraid she was about to pick his teeth clean. She's a wild one, I can tell."

I nod her way just as Annette snatches a couple of napkins off the nearest table and wipes herself clean.

"Here, let me help," I say, stealing a napkin myself and dabbing her dress.

"No, it's fine." She pushes me away as she surveys the area. "Oh shoot. I lost him. He was a looker, too. If you see the hot man with deep blue eyes, stay away. He's mine."

"Oh right." I give a nervous laugh as I glance around, hoping Everett has made a mad rush for the car.

Gemma brays out another laugh. "She's a comedian! Put her in her place, Lottie. I knew a girl like her back in my corral days. I'd spit on her if I could."

As much as I'd like to oblige Gemma, I decide to go at it from another direction.

"Hey? I think we've met before. You're Aspen's friend. We met the night of the charity event."

She rolls her eyes. "He just brought that up, too. Isn't that weird? We were both there. I think maybe we're meant to be together. The universe just keeps throwing us at one another. I saw him this morning, too, at some ridiculous book club. My goodness, they don't make them any hotter than Noah Boxer."

Noah Boxer? Good cover, Everett.

"Isn't it terrible what happened to Trisha Maples that night? Can you believe someone shot her right there in the parking lot? In fact, I think she had just finished introducing us right before it happened."

She sucks in a breath. Her eyes widen with horror as she scans the room as if suddenly looking for an exit.

Gemma clip-clops in close to her. “Oh, she’s guilty, Lottie. I can see it in her scheming eyes. Should we trample her now?”

I shake my head over at the eager llama anxious to cause some serious bodily harm to our very first suspect.

Annette leans my way. “That’s right. She did introduce us.” She shudders a moment. “Trisha knew my aunt. I’ve had to listen to my aunt Gerrie complain about that woman for years. Of course, I worked with Trisha, too. We all volunteer down at the shelter.” Her eyes flit to the left, and I can tell she’s getting twitchy. “Have they arrested him yet?”

“Arrested who?” both Gemma and I say in unison.

“Leo—her boyfriend. Everyone knows they’ve had a rocky relationship. I knew it was a matter of time before he left her, but I had no idea he’d shove her off the planet.”

My hand clutches to my chest. “Why in the world would he do that?”

“I don’t know, but he’s guilty. He writes murder mysteries for a living. You would think he could get a little more creative on how to kill someone.” She starts to take off. “Oh, and hey, you run that bakery, right?”

“Yes, the Cutie Pie Bakery and Cakery.”

Gemma groans, “Great. A woman like this only wants something for free.”

“Would you want to donate a few pies to the shelter this Thanksgiving? You could drop them off in the morning and you won’t have to miss out on your own celebration.”

"Ah-ha! I knew it. She wants pies, Lottie. She's only using you for your pies," Gemma cries out. "Actually, that was pretty thoughtful, wasn't it?"

I nod covertly at the beast with the good hair.

Annette is making it awfully hard to not like her. Clearly, she's a good person. She volunteers at a homeless shelter *and* she's helping to score some of my pies to help feed them on Thanksgiving? It would seem she truly is a good person. But plenty of good people have been convicted of murder before, so there's that.

"I would love to," I say. "In fact, I'm not only going to volunteer my pies, I'm going to volunteer myself. I don't mind one bit helping out with serving the food."

"Perfect. Show up as early as you want and stay as late as you like. Even an hour of help is huge." She sighs as she inspects the crowd. "I'd better get back to work. What was your name again?"

As tempted as I am to slip her an alias, I go with the truth. "Lottie Lemon. It's nice to get to know you, Annette."

"It's Nettie." She wrinkles her nose. "Who knows? If I land that hottie from Honey Hollow, we might just be seeing more of each other. Ta-ta for now!"

"Ta-ta," I say as I glance around for said hottie.

Gemma's enormous body begins to sway to the music once again. Her neck moves to and fro as her feet tap to the beat. "Pardon me, Lottie. Now that our work is done, it's time for this llama mama to have some fun." She sashays her way to the dance floor once again.

"Goodbye, Gemma!" I call out just as Keelie comes over to collect what's left of her drink.

"Come on, Lottie. You owe me a dance." And I give it to her.

Keelie, Lily, Naomi, and I dance up a storm and Cormack joins us for a few songs before we call it a night and hunt down our respective dates.

I find Everett at the end of the bar.

"I apologize," I say, still trying to catch my breath.

"For what? Having a good time?" He wraps his arms around me and gives my cheek a quick peck. "By the way, I checked online and it's totally safe for a woman in your condition to shake her stuff on the dance floor."

A laugh titters from me. "Why thank you, Dr. Baxter. I'm glad to have your clearance," I tease, shaking my head up at him in wonder. "I love how you love me."

He dips down and presses a kiss to my ear. "I love you both."

"I know you do."

He pulls back, his expression suddenly all too serious. "Why don't we drive by the hospital on the way home? I know it's past visiting hours, but I happen to have an in with the nurses." He gives a quick wink. "Let's tell Noah he needs to fight like never before. We still need him."

Everett and I do just that.

I hope Noah heard.

I hope he feels loved and needed. Because that's exactly what we told him. And it's the truth.

The baby and I need him more than ever before.

10

Exhaustion has set in.

Everett and I have been reading those baby books as if they were instruction manuals on what our future holds—and I suppose they are. Last night Everett sweetly brought me Wicked Wok *and* a Mangias pizza in the event I craved both. He even went out and bought me a brand new pair of comfy PJs that make me feel as if I'm sleeping in a fluffy pink cloud.

I can't imagine Everett taking time out of his busy life to head into a store to buy clothes for me, but it was extremely thoughtful of him.

He's still spending the night at my place with his arms wrapped around me tight, and, in truth, I don't know if I could sleep without him anymore.

But all day, every minute, my mind drifts to Noah and our baby. This should be the happiest time of our lives.

Instead, he's fighting for his life, and I'm lying in bed at night with his former stepbrother.

A part of me wants to delve into the dark what-ifs.

What if Noah doesn't survive?

It would be the end of everything. I couldn't bear it. The pain alone might kill me.

On a practical note, I'm sure Everett and I would make our relationship official once again. We would probably get married as soon as possible, and Everett would raise this baby as if it were his own. And, eventually, I would have Everett's biological child, too. Most likely many of them, considering the stock we're dealing with. Of course, I feel that way about Noah, too.

Oh, how I hate exploring the labyrinth my heart has become.

The Cutie Pie Bakery and Cakery just finished with its morning rush. My mother sits in the corner with Carlotta, both of them working up a storm. My mother is busy writing her book and Carlotta seems to be recording her with her phone as if documenting the event. I don't pretend to understand Carlotta. I simply try to stay out of her way.

"Lottie?" Lily trots to the registers where I'm standing, holding up a book in her hand. "What is this doing in your tote bag? *Make Room for Baby*?"

I do a double take at that rectangular piece of literature and dive over it in haste.

"Give me that." I'm quick to wrestle it from her.

"No!" Lily is tenacious. "I can't believe you've been holding a secret so big. You and Everett are about to become parents! Poor Noah. That didn't take long, did it?"

I grunt and twist and finally come up the victor.

"Lottie?" Mom calls from the other end of the counter, and I quickly shove the book up the back of my sweater.

She's wearing a silk cranberry-colored blouse that just so happens to be unbuttoned enough to show off far too much of her décolleté than necessary.

Carlotta steps in next to her and cranes her neck in my direction. She smirks down at my hidden hand and nods because she knows I'm up to no good.

"What can I help you ladies with?" I blink over at them with the upmost professionalism.

Mom waves me off. "We're headed to the library. I've got a writers group that starts in ten minutes. My *how to write a murder* club has procured a local author to come in and speak with us today. He's going to teach us how to pull off the perfect crime." Her brows waggle, and her voice is low and husky when she says that last part as if it were sexually provocative, and knowing my mother it will be.

"That's great. How about some cookies to take over with you? I'm sure Lainey wouldn't mind." Lainey is the head librarian down at the Honey Hollow Library, and outside of the two of us, I don't think there's another soul in the world who loves their career choice more than she does. As a little girl, Lainey was always surrounded with books. And as a little girl, I was always surrounded with cake batter. Our little sister, Meg, was surrounded with boys she liked to beat up.

Mom nods. “Cookies would be perfect.”

Carlotta twitches her nose at my mother. “Let’s hope he’s a hottie. After Topper dumped you, I’m rooting you find a decent man fast. You know what they say. The quickest way to get over a man is to get under another one.”

Lily laughs, but I groan at the thought, partially because it happens to be a mantra my mother has subscribed to many, many times before.

Mom scoffs. “Oh, Carlotta, Topper didn’t dump me. In fact, we’re having dinner tomorrow night at the B&B to straighten this whole mess out. He’s assured me it’s nothing but a misunderstanding.”

Carlotta grunts, “I don’t know, Miranda. This murder mystery guru sounds like a beast of a man. With a name like Leo Workman, how can he not be? I bet he roars like a lion when he—”

“Okay!” I say, taking a breath and then holding it abruptly. “Wait, Carlotta, did you say Leo Workman?” My mind flits back to the night of the murder. He introduced himself to me that night as Trisha’s steady Eddie—right before he dragged her off. It looked like they were squabbling. When I spoke to Annette, she mentioned they were on the rocks, and that he probably did it. She said he wrote murder mysteries for a living! My goodness, this is the same person. "You know what? Why don't you ladies skip on ahead? I'm going to bring a platter full of pumpkin spiced goodies down myself. In fact, I'm going to sit in on your group if you don't mind. I'm thinking about writing a book myself."

Lily giggles. "Yeah, Lottie is really interested in books as of late." She gives a hard knock over that book shoved against my back and I shoot her a look.

Mom nods while pressing her fingers to her all too exposed chest. "Oh, you should, Lottie. I'm finding it so cathartic. And it would be for you, too. Just make a list of all the people you'd like to kill and then fictionalize it." She leans in hard. "I've already killed off half of Honey Hollow." A gritty giggle pumps from her. "We'll see you there."

Carlotta waves from the door. "Bring some pumpkin spiced blondies, and I might save you a seat."

"Lily, man the fort," I say, hustling my baby book back into the office before quickly throwing together a box of every pumpkin spiced goodie I can find. "I'm headed off to solve a mystery."

The Honey Hollow Library is tucked up on a quiet street. The parking lot is sparsely filled as a smattering of women head on in with toddlers and babies alike. I balance the box of sweets in my hand while my other hand goes straight to my belly as if responding to some innate maternal cue.

The brunette up ahead of me holds open the door for her tiny brood, a little girl with dark braids and a young boy with an adorable baseball cap. Those could be my children with Noah—my children with *Everett* for that matter. They're so tiny and precious I could stare at them forever.

"You too." She hitches her head my way, and I quicken my steps to accommodate her for holding the door open for me.

"Thank you," I say.

"No problem." She glances down to my hand still protectively sealed over Noah's sweet child. "When's your baby due?"

I gasp as I do a quick scan of the vicinity. "Um, I'm not really sure. I just found out. I haven't really seen the doctor yet. In fact, I'm still trying to find a good one."

"Dr. Barnette," she says as if it were the only choice. "She's the best of the best, and she has an office right here in town. She delivered all of my babies for me so far, and I have another one due in August. I just found out myself, and I still haven't broken the news to my husband. I've been scrolling Pinterest in hopes to get super creative. You know you have to stage these things, and every announcement has to be more outlandish than the last. Heaven forbid you get accused of stealing the idea from someone in one of your mommy groups." She groans as she looks to the ceiling. "Mommy cliques are the worst. Hey? You're probably due in August, too. Have fun with it. And remember Dr. Barnette!" She trots off after her children who have already sailed on toward the library proper.

The expansive foyer boasts a vaulted ceiling that shoots up fifty feet at least and gives the library a grand appeal.

Outside of the scent of something delicious baking in the oven, the next best way to intoxicate my senses is with books. I take in the sweet scent of pulp, and it takes me right back to my youth where my mother carted us off to the library every chance she had.

I take a moment to peruse the colorful décor in the foyer. Artwork from local students lines the walls, and it adds a homey feel to this already homey structure that holds a special place in my heart.

Inside, the thick carpeting dampens the sound of footfalls as a handful of people mill around the new books section.

And sure enough, seated behind the wide checkout desk are Lainey and one of her coworkers, Laurie Ackerman, who just had a baby last year.

I head over and open up my box of goodies. "Morning, ladies! First treat of the day goes to the two of you for keeping order in the stacks."

Laurie quickly dips a hand into the box and comes up victorious with a pumpkin scone, but Lainey picks up a children's picture book next to her and places it over her nose instead.

My sister pinches her nose shut while squinting as if she might be sick.

"Oh goodness, get that thing away from me."

"*Lainey*, are you saying my cookies stink?"

"I'm saying the box stinks."

Both Laurie and I ogle my sister as if she just sprouted a second head.

"Fine. I'll be joining the mystery crew if you need any more cookies," I say to both of them and her coworker gives me the thumbs-up.

I trot off and spot a large crowd congregating around a table, all women about my mother's age.

Carlotta waves me over and I head that way.

Everyone here has either a laptop or a stack of notebooks spread out before them, and here all I brought were cookies.

Mom sits right next to a rather handsome older man, chatting away with him in her effort to become the teacher's plaything, no doubt. And low and behold, he's the exact man I met that night. A tingle of excitement rides through me at the thought of walking right into another suspect this morning.

Ha! And Ivy can't do a thing about it because this one just so happens to be teaching a class on all things—murder.

A familiar brunette looks up on the other side of Carlotta, and I do a double take.

"Meg?" I trot her way and land the cookies in the center of the table, inviting everyone to partake, and soon enough ten hands have already dipped into the tiny pink box.

Carlotta scoots over a notch, and I land between her and my sister.

"Meg, what are you doing here?" I whisper.

"Mom inspired me to write a murder mystery of my own. I'm thinking strippers who kill bad tippers. Then I can move on to waitresses and parking valets who kill the cheapest of the cheap. I'll call it the *Tipping Point Series*."

"It sounds riveting," I say as Carlotta sticks a finger down her throat behind my sister's back.

Carlotta looks startlingly like me in this soft light, and a part of me wants to tell her to knock off the bad attitude. I'm an ardent encourager of both my sisters' hopes and dreams, be they wrestling in an oil pit or teaching dirty dancers their night moves. I would never vomit on their big ideas.

"Am I late?" a shrill female voice warbles from somewhere up above, and I turn to find Gemma in all her luscious llama glory clip-clopping her way over. Her neck juts back and forth with her every step, and those extreme lashes of hers instantly mesmerize me. She's such a cutie and a hoot to boot. I'd like to keep her around forever. Come to think of it, I always say that about the ghosts that visit, but it never happens—with the exception of Greer. For reasons beyond my control of understanding, the ghost of Greer Giles lives on to haunt my mother's B&B. And believe you me, my mother's bottom line is grateful.

I shake my head over at Gemma and she offers an adorable wink.

"Ooh"—she moans with glee—"look at this one, Lottie."

Leo stands for a brief moment and bows to all the faces rapt at attention. His silver hair is thick and cropped short. He has a leathery look about him, deeply tanned as if he spends most of his time outdoors. And that peppering of silver stubble over his cheeks gives him a rugged appeal.

"Welcome, everyone." He falls back into his seat with a grin blooming on his face. He's affable, I'll give him that, and if I'm not mistaken, most every woman here is swooning in his direction.

"My name is Leo Workman, writer of mystery—lover of murder." His grin broadens as a quiet round of titters circles the table. "My critically acclaimed series *Killing Your Darling* has become an international bestseller, and I've been nominated for three Silver Hatchet awards, the highest accolade in the mystery writing world." A light applause breaks out. "Let's do a quick round of introductions. Tell me your name and a little about the book you're working on." He nods to the lady on his left, and Mom openly frowns.

Seeing she's on his right, she'll be last. I'm learning a bit more about my mother as time goes by and, I'll have Leo Workman know, my mother doesn't like playing second, third, or fifteenth fiddle to anyone. Let's call a spade a spade. Had he nodded in her direction first, he might have gotten lucky.

Gemma scoots in across the table from me and sits on the ground. Her long neck dips between the two women on the end as if she were a student.

One by one each woman introduces herself, and, sure enough, we hear every outlandish plot idea under the terrifying sun. Looking for a meals-on-wheels murder? We've got one. Death by ice cream? It's happening. An icepick wielding serial killer who stalks men who have recently been paroled for traffic tickets? It's on.

Soon enough, it's Meg's turn and she unleashes her killer strippers into the wild and is met with a murmuring round of approval.

Leo nods my way. He's smiling so hard, rows of laugh lines heavily embed themselves around his eyes.

"And you?"

"I—uh..." I glance around and every pair of eyes here is feasted upon me, waiting for me to regale them with my murderous work in progress.

Carlotta jabs me hard in the ribs. "Lottie and I are co-writing a book together."

"Oh!" Mom jumps in her seat. "That's so wonderful." She claps hard as if it warmed her heart a thousand degrees to see the two of us collaborating on anything, which makes me question whether or not she's met the real Carlotta yet.

A dark laugh pumps from the demon to my left as Carlotta leans in. "It's about a baker who can see the dead."

She couldn't have surprised me more if she kicked me in the gut. I roll my eyes at her lack of creativity.

The table lights up with a round of *oohs and ahs*, and it sounds as if a ghost were already among us—Gemma withstanding.

"Yup"—Carlotta is proving to be unstoppable—"and get this! She sees pets that have come back from the other side, and they're always a bad omen for their previous owners."

A woman on the end clutches at her chest. "What happens to the previous owner?"

Carlotta runs her finger along her neck, pretending to slash it, and the entire table gasps.

Insert eye roll number two.

"I see." Leo sounds markedly impressed. I swear, if he steals our idea, I'm suing and maybe siccing a ghost or two on him. "And what's the plotline of your current work?"

Carlotta leans in. "It's about a murder mystery writer who shot his girlfriend in cold blood at the Evergreen *Inn*."

"Oh goodness," I groan. Kill me.

Leo closes his eyes a moment. "Ah, I do see where this is going." His affect changes on a dime. "Why don't we get this right out in the open?" He offers Carlotta an affable smile. "Yes, I was dating a woman who was recently killed. No, I did not commit this crime. The sheriff's department is working very hard to locate the person who is responsible for this heinous atrocity. In fact, I was contacted just yesterday afternoon and told they have a very strong lead in the case. Since I was familiar with the person they were implicating, I provided all the information they needed on the perpetrator. So, as you can see, I am in full compliance with the investigation, and I'm certain the killer will be apprehended shortly." He nods to Carlotta. "Rest assured, you are not in the presence of someone who could do such a terrible thing. The only killing I ever get around to is strictly on paper."

Honestly? Me thinks the award-winning novelist doth protest too much.

Gemma bats her lashes my way. "What do you think, Lottie? Has that detective got a serious lead?"

I shrug over at her. Ivy won't tell me a thing. But why would she confide in Leo? It doesn't make sense.

He finishes off the getting-to-know-you circle with a nod to my mother.

"Miranda Lemon." She gives a cheeky wink to the crowd. "Some of you might know me. I own and operate the Haunted Honey Hollow Inn." She chortles his way as if this were a selling point in their budding relationship. And, judging by the way his brows just hiked up a notch, it might be. "My novel is about a woman who hacks to pieces all the philandering boyfriends in her life. And there might be a control freak in there, too, for good measure." She bubbles with a quiet laugh, and Meg kicks me from under the table.

"Knew it," she whispers my way. "Mom has been knocking off her plus ones and you've been covering for her. Good work, Lot. If Hook ever wanders, I'll know who to come to for help."

Good grief.

Leo starts in about the writing craft in general. He teaches us how to outline, set manageable goals for ourselves, and how to delve deep and uncover the complex motives for murder.

He generously dissects his latest novel in which a woman by the name of Trista, a volunteer at a woman's shelter, is gunned down in an alley after threatening to leave her boyfriend of one year.

Huh. That doesn't sound so complex. In fact, Trista sounds a lot like *Trisha*—who happens to be a volunteer at a *homeless* shelter. I knew Leo would prove to be fishy. This has truth-is-stranger-than-fiction written all over it.

An hour drifts by and the group disbands, leaving only crumbs in my little pink box of goodies.

Bodies drift from the table as Gemma walks right through it, only to stop in the middle, and it's an unnerving sight.

Carlotta knocks me in the ribs with her elbow. "Get a load of this one."

"Would you hush? Gemma is a sweetheart."

Gemma brays out a gentle laugh. "I think very highly of you, too, Lottie. But I can't say the same about Leo the Liar. He's a killer, Lottie. He's practically laid out how and why he slaughtered poor Trisha in cold blood. How could that bumbling detective look at anyone besides him?"

"Maybe she really does have hard evidence on someone else?" I shrug over at her. "I'll see if I can find out." I tick my head his way.

Gemma scoffs. "I don't think he can spell it out any clearer if he tried. And no offense to this scholastic environment, but I much prefer dancing. Here's a thought. Try to corner your next suspect in the vicinity of some good music. I always did like to shake my tail at the boys in the barn."

Carlotta leans in. "Sounds like you and Lottie have a lot in common."

"Oh hush." I all but swat her.

Leo is quickly packing up, and my mother is bending his ear at the speed of light so I head on over in an effort to ironically save him.

"Great class," I say enthusiastically. "You really gave some good insight on how to write a novel. I especially liked the part about creating our own Kanban boards. I'm a big list maker, so that only seems like a natural progression."

"Oh, you'll love it then." His eyes widen a notch, and I note they're an arresting shade of silver. I can see the appeal that would draw my mother like a fly to Honey Hollow Honey, but this silver fox just might happen to be a murderer. And a murderer who specializes in killing ex-girlfriends? Some might say he and my mother are the perfect murderous pair. But given the choice, I much prefer her with a philandering cheat looking for a naughty good time like Topper. At least I know the worst Topper can do is break her heart—not stop it.

"Oh, wait." I stretch the words out a little too long. "I think I met you the night of the charity event. You were standing with Trisha."

His lids lower a notch. "Ah, yes, the baker. The one who sees the dead, I'm guessing?" A dry laugh pumps from him.

Funny. For a guy who just lost the love of his life, he sure is in a great mood.

"That's right," I say and his expression sobers up on a dime.

Carlotta calls my mother and she quickly excuses herself.

I lean in and whisper, "So, who does the sheriff's department think did this? I mean, you're obviously not a killer. You're a fiction writer. And Trisha adored you. I could see it in her eyes." Nothing like an ego stroke to bring the suspects to the yard.

His own eyes twinkle at the thought. "She did, didn't she?" He gives a wistful shake of the head. "And I adored my Trish-Trish. We had plans to travel to the Mediterranean this summer. I was set to propose, but she'll never know that. I gave her daughter the ring. I couldn't keep it. And, in my heart, it already belonged to Trisha."

"Her daughter? Was that the young brunette? Jade something?"

"No." He shakes his head quickly. "Jade Pope was her assistant. Her daughter's name is Chanelle Maples. I'm afraid they were estranged. But, oddly enough, that's how I met her mother. Chanelle and I were going through AA together a little over a year ago and Trisha showed up one night to support her. The two of us just hit it off. And, for the record, I haven't hit a bottle in going on thirty-two months."

"Congratulations," I say it low and quiet because it doesn't feel right congratulating him on anything.

"I appreciate that."

I suck in a contrived breath as I do my best to feign surprise. "Is that who they think did it? Her estranged daughter?"

"No." He glances around before leaning in so close I can count the whiskers on his chin. "They think this was all brought about by a falling-out she had with her friend Gerrie."

"The older woman? The volunteer from the shelter?"

He nods.

"Why in the world would she gun down Trisha in the parking lot? And for some reason, I can't see her with a gun at all."

He shrugs. "I'm afraid I've said too much already." He takes off after my mother and he has her giggling like a schoolgirl before they ever hit the exit.

Trisha has an estranged daughter. *Huh.*

But Leo says that the sheriff's department is sniffing around Gerrie.

Interesting.

However, he's the one who wrote a how-to book on how to slaughter an ex.

I really do think he's deflecting too much.

For my mother's sake, let's hope she isn't getting involved with yet another monster.

And if she is, she can kill him in her very next book.

Or I can kill him.

I've done it before.

11

Later that night, Alex lets me know that he and his mother will be having dinner at my mother's B&B where she'll be staying, and he kindly invited both Everett and me to join them.

The B&B is adorable and homey inside. It houses a number of rooms upstairs and has been steadily filled with tourists thanks to the pack of ghosts haunting these halls. The entry is huge and expansive, and you can see the fireplace roaring in both the dining room and the grand room from that vantage point. My mother recently had a conservatory tacked onto the back, a large glass room that's played host to many gatherings. And, unfortunately, many a murders, too.

Everett and I arrive together, and I must say he looks particularly handsome tonight. His hair is getting a little longer in the back, his eyes look brighter, and I think there's a spring in his step.

"Everett, you not only look amazing tonight, but I feel like your energy is different. If I didn't know better, I'd think you were a man with a secret."

The tips of his lips curl with satisfaction. "I am, Lemon." He leans in and brazenly lands a kiss to my lips. "We both have a secret."

I nod up at him, tears sparkling in my eyes at the thought of this baby putting a spring in Judge Baxter's step.

"Our baby," I whisper. I did say *our* and I meant it. I know that Everett will be in this child's life in a very important way whether or not Noah pulls through. But Noah is pulling through. I'll find a way to make that happen if I have to.

A brilliant spray of stars appears before us with the power of a supernova, and soon enough Gemma is standing before us.

"Did you say our baby?" Gemma's mouth opens wide and her prominent bottom teeth buck in all sorts of crazy directions. "Lottie, are you and Everett having a baby?"

"*Ooh*"—a dull moan comes from me as if I'm about to be sick and I might—"you can't say a word about the baby to Noah. This might actually kill him." I don't know why I didn't deny it, but a part of me doesn't have the heart to lie to the ghost of a llama—mostly. And, technically, this very much is Everett's baby, too.

"Oh, Lottie." Gemma does a little tap dance, her neck bobbling back and forth. "This is fantastic news. A baby is the best of the best. I've had twenty-three of them myself."

Carlotta pops up like the ghost of mothers past. "Who's having a baby?" She gasps as she glances down at my stomach, and I follow her gaze, only to find my hand absentmindedly strapped to my belly.

"Not me!" I'm quick to shout it out like a war cry. "Everett? Why don't you head into the conservatory to see if Alex and Suze are there? I'll be right over."

He leans in. "Good luck putting out this fire." He dots my cheek with a kiss before taking off.

I turn to Carlotta and pull her in by the sweater. "Lainey is having the baby and don't you dare ruin this. She hasn't broken the news yet to Forest or my mother." GAH! Mother of all lies! But, it wouldn't be the first time I've accidentally on purpose started rumors about my sweet sister.

She squints over at me. "She didn't tell the hubby? And yet she told the one sister who she thinks is a broken mirror personified?" Carlotta inspects me with a scrutinizing gaze. "Interesting."

The ghost of a little girl stalks up with her long, stringy hair combed over her face, a dirty pinafore paired with a scruffy pair of Mary Janes on her feet, and a bloody hatchet dangling from one hand.

"Lea!" I perk up at the sight of her. Little Azalea, *Lea*, had her family slaughtered right over the grounds of the B&B many, many moons ago, and she's been haunting the area ever since, right along with her adoptive parents, Greer Giles and Winslow Decker.

"Lottie, is that you?" Lea hitches her hair behind her ear, and her pretty dark eyes stare up at me. "I've got big news for you. A real surprise."

Carlotta lets out a husky laugh. "Lottie's got a pretty big surprise, too." She scowls over at me. "I'm not buying that knocked-up sister story of yours. But don't worry. I'm really good at singing the baby blues. It's a tune I'm all too familiar with."

Dear Lord. Carlotta is like a walking minefield with this delicate information.

"What's this?" Little Lea magically appears on Gemma's back, and she kicks her heels into the fuzzy girl's sides. "Lottie, are you having a baby? Let it be known, I hate the wailing creatures. I simply loathe them."

I make a face at her. "Nobody hates babies, Lea. They're adorable. And you're going to love mine because it will be the most precious thing you've ever laid your dead little eyes on."

"*Ah-ha*!" Carlotta claps her hands together. "I knew it! Miranda is gonna be a granny!"

I roll my eyes because Carlotta conveniently left herself out of the granny equation.

"Don't worry, Lot." She pats me on the back. "I won't tell many people."

Mayor Nash walks in through the door and offers a cheery greeting just as Carlotta zips off in his direction.

"You won't believe what your darling, yet loose, little daughter has up and gotten herself into."

They speed off to the conservatory where I'll be in just a moment to hang Carlotta by her toes.

"Lottie?" Lea calls as Gemma dances her in a circle. "Guess what my surprise is?"

"A noose you'd like for me to put to good use with Carlotta?" I glance back, only to find the ghost of a familiar looking black cat in little Lea's arms. "Thirteen!" I say with marked enthusiasm as I head over and offer his fur a quick scratch. Thirteen is a jet-black cat whose fur sparkles with onyx-colored stars, his eyes glow a brilliant shade of green, and he just so happened to be the spirit sent to help solve last month's murder. "How is this possible? Don't tell me I left a killer on the loose? Or worse yet, Pastor Gaines has managed to resurrect himself."

That would be a true and frightening nightmare.

"Heavens no." His whiskers twitch in the same way my cats are prone to do when they're feeling snippy. "He's dead and gone, and I'm dead and here. It turns out, since the killer and the deceased were one and the same in my case, I was able to put in for an extension."

"Oh, that's wonderful." A part of me wonders if Noah will be able to put in an extension, if for some reason he doesn't make it. And suddenly, I feel crestfallen just thinking about it. "Well, I, for one, am thrilled you'll be staying on. And I know Lea is glad about it, too. I'd better get into the conservatory. I'm late for dinner with my brand new mother-in-law."

Lea laughs. "Lottie is eating for two. She's having a baby."

"Lord," I groan. "Lea, don't tell Greer, whatever you do. She's a terrible gossip." A dead one nevertheless. Her mouth still reigns supreme in that sense.

Gemma trots off to the delight of both Lea and Thirteen, and I quickly make my way into the conservatory.

The conservatory is light and bright, sparsely populated with guests who all seem to be taking their meals in here this evening. You can't blame them. My mother has lit up the woods outside of these glass walls with twinkle lights, and it lends for a dramatic backdrop. It really does feel as if you're enjoying your meal in the middle of the woods, sans the icy cold air of autumn and the potential black bear ruining your fun and perhaps your life.

Carlotta and Mayor Nash are laughing it up over something to my right, and I can't help but make a face. Mayor Nash waves me over.

"Congrats, Lottie! I won't say a word." He pretends to zip his lips, and I quickly drift away from them as if they were diseased.

Good grief. I'm going to have to break this to Noah before he hears it from somebody else.

A few tables over I spot my mother and Topper Blakley having what looks to be an intimate yet slightly heated conversation, and I don't dare go near them with a ten-foot baby. I mean pole. Why did I say *baby*?

I glance down to find my hand settled over my stomach again.

GAH!

I pull it away as if it were embedded in flames.

"Leland!" a woman hisses from behind, and I turn to find Britney looking particularly enraged. A blonde curl cleverly hides her left eye, but the rest of her face speaks angry volumes. "She's here."

"Who's here?" And then it hits me. "Oh, that's right, I keep forgetting Suze was your mother-in-law far before she ever was mine." I step back and iron out the front of my dress. "What do you think? Do I look okay?" I don't wear dresses on the regular, but I pulled out a cranberry corduroy number I found hiding in the back of my closet. And I managed to dig up a matching pair of suede boots that hike over my knees, meeting it at its hemline.

"You look like a slutty pilgrim. But never mind you." She cranes her neck behind me. "Geez, she is here. What's that wicked witch doing in Honey Hollow anyway? Has Noah finally kicked the bucket?"

I swat her on the arm. "Don't you dare put that out in the universe. No, he's not dead. And he will never be dead. Noah is going to live forever."

She rolls her eyes at the thought. "That will be a first."

"Yes, it will. Now, if you weren't talking about Suze, who were you talking about?"

She wrinkles her nose. "Call her Suzanna. She loves that more than anything."

"Very funny, but I've already been warned not to. So, spill it. Who's the infamous she?"

Britney glances to the left, and I follow her gaze, only to find Finn and Naomi laughing it up at a secluded table.

"Oh my goodness?" I gasp. "Does that boy have no sense?"

Britney grunts, "I'm beginning to wonder the same thing. I'm sorry, Lorena, but I don't tolerate threesomes the way you do. I'm afraid I'm going to have to break it off with your brother." She lifts her chin stoically. "We had a good run."

"No, don't do that. I'm sure there's a perfectly good explanation. Go over there and douse Naomi with water and I'm sure Finn will give it to you."

Everett waves to me from the back, and I spot him there with Alex and a blonde woman with short hair that swoops to the side. She's wearing a tight red dress that makes the getup I've donned look like it belongs on a nun, and I can hear her booming laugh clear across the room.

Here it goes. I'm about to meet Noah's mother, my mother-in-law.

My heart rate picks up as I make my way over, and soon I'm standing right before the three of them breathless with my hand extended.

"Lottie Lemon," I say, noting how identical her eyes are to Noah's, and her dimples are digging in on either side of her cheeks just like they do with both her handsome boys. She's pretty, beautiful, in fact, and yet she seems—I guess *livid* would be the word I'm looking for. "I'm Noah's wife."

The smile dissipates from her face and she shakes her head at me.

"So, you're next in line to suck the money out of my son's bank account. I'd say glad to meet you, but I don't think either of us wants to start this relationship off with a lie. I suppose you'll join us. Alex and Everett have been speaking highly of you, and it makes me wonder what they're hiding from me." Her emerald green eyes flit to Alex. "Is she a killer?"

"Nope." Alex doesn't miss a beat. "But she has a penchant for tracking them down."

I shoot Everett a look as I take a seat between him and Alex. It's safe to say Suze and I didn't exactly get off on the right foot, but that's on her. I came in as nice as can be. And will remain so. I think.

A dark laugh brews in Everett's chest as he picks up my hand. "Don't worry, Lemon. Her bark is worse than her bite. Isn't that right, Suze?"

She huffs over at him. "You're lucky I like you, Everett. And why are the two of you holding hands? Let me guess. My poor son isn't in the ground yet and you've already 'Essexed' her."

I roll my eyes. Everett's true formal name is Essex, but the only people he allows to call him by his proper moniker are those he's bedded. It's sort of a door prize they come away with after the main mattress event. With the exception, of course, of his mother and sister who have only referred to him as Essex since the day he was born. It's more or less a well-known fact, thus Suze's peculiar knowledge of the name game. I, however, prefer to call him by the name I've known him as from the beginning. And lucky for me, Everett doesn't mind one bit.

Everett shakes his head. "Nope. Lemon and I were dating before they got hitched."

I lean in, indignant. "And they're not putting Noah in the ground. He's going to pull through."

She presses out a manufactured smile. "I like a woman who chooses to hold strong to her delusions." Her features smooth out once again as if solidifying to iron. "But these are the wrong delusions to cling to." Her blood red nails tap against the sides of her glass. "I just came from a visit and I used to be a nurse. I know exactly what his odds are. But don't you worry. As his wife, you'll be the recipient of all his earthly belongings. I'm sure that last wife of his is kicking herself for not holding strong another few months." She does a double take to her left. "And there's the nitwit who was driving the car."

I turn around, and sure enough Cormack is seated with both my mother and Topper. Oddly enough, the conversation they're embroiled in looks as if it's escalating.

Perfect. That's exactly what this night needs, a Featherheaded crescendo.

Alex clears his throat. "Lottie has a bakery on Main Street. Maybe tomorrow after we visit Noah we can stop by?"

Suze snorts. "And fill myself with empty carbs? No, thank you."

A member of my mother's waitstaff drops off the dinner menu, and we quickly peruse it before putting in our orders. I can't help but note that Suze chose the pasta carbonara with garlic breadsticks and mashed potatoes, an empty carb trifecta, but I'll be the last to point that out to her.

"So, Suze?" I struggle to make eye contact with her, and if I didn't know better, I'd think she was ignoring me. "What keeps you busy?"

"Are you implying I'm diddling away my time? I'll have you know that not all women of a certain age sit around baking cookies all day, trying to ply them off on people."

My mouth falls open. Was that a slight dig at me? I'm not of a certain age, am I?

I decide to take the high road and change the subject. "Both Everett and I have been visiting Noah daily. We're both confident he'll come back to us. We talk to him. And we just know he can hear us, so we try to keep it positive."

"Oh, he can't hear you." Suze is quick to blow it off. "He's lost in a deep slumber. He doesn't know a darn thing that's happened to him. That's the saving grace in all of this."

I glance to Everett because we happen to know otherwise.

Everett nods over to her. "How long does Honey Hollow have the honor of your presence, Suze?"

She smiles over at him and it looks genuine. "I'll be here until just after Thanksgiving, and then I'm off to a cruise in the Aegean. I'm afraid I have a non-refundable ticket. Whatever will be with my son, will be. He would never want me to miss this trip, despite his destiny."

"That's true," a warm voice whispers into my ear and I jump, only to turn around and see a handsome poltergeist that has hijacked my heart and my womb.

"Noah!" I gasp, filled with relief, and then immediately with regret.

"Excuse me?" Suze doesn't look amused by my little outburst.

"I mean, yes, that sounds exactly like Noah." I give Everett's hand a squeeze because I know he heard Noah's voice, too.

Suze eyes our conjoined hands and sighs hard. "The two of you visit my son, and then let me guess, you jump into bed together in an effort to comfort one another?" She says *comfort* with air quotes and Noah chuckles.

"What are you laughing at?" I whisper.

Suze shakes her head. "Oh, I'm not laughing. You're lucky I like you, Everett. But haven't you and Noah had enough of one another's leftovers? What does your mother think of all this? You do know I highly admire Eliza and respect her opinion."

"My mother loves her." Everett shrugs as if he can't explain it.

Gee thanks.

Suze gags on her next caustic thoughts.

Noah leans in. "There she goes. She's trying to rewire her brain to do the same. But don't worry. She only likes a handful of people. The important thing is that I love you, Lottie. Don't think twice about whatever it is that's about to pop out of her mouth. She doesn't have a filter, if you hadn't noticed."

"Oh, I noticed."

Everett nods as if agreeing with me.

"*Huh.*" She takes a breath while appraising me again for the very first time. "Maybe I will have to stop by your bakery. Noah loved my chocolate chip cookies growing up. I'll have to see if they're anywhere as good as I used to make them."

The sharp cry of a woman explodes to our left, and we turn to find Naomi standing up, dripping with what looks to be spaghetti sauce from head to toe.

I see Britney chose to forgo the water bath I suggested and went for the Bolognese gold.

"You *witch*!" Naomi launches at Britney, and Finn does his best to stave them off.

"I'd better take care of this." Alex bounds over and plucks Naomi off of her victim and carries her right out of the conservatory.

"And, it looks as if Naomi got exactly what she wanted all along," I say before turning to Suze. "Naomi is in love with your son."

"Well, I certainly don't approve." A sarcastic laugh booms from her. "He'll have to try again, much like Noah." She averts her eyes.

Noah groans, "Feel free to leave, Lottie. You don't need to put up with this."

Everett sighs in the woman's direction. "Suze, do you really want to fracture a relationship with the love of Noah's life?"

Her eyes soften for a moment as tears begin to glitter in them. She opens her mouth to say something just as the sound of wild cackling bursts from our right, and I look back to find both Cormack and my mother sitting in Topper's lap.

"Oh no, you don't." I'm about to get up when Cormack spontaneously evicts herself and slaps Topper across the face. "Good Lord." At least one of them has common sense.

She picks up her purse and makes a beeline in this direction.

Noah moans, "And here we go."

She falls into Alex's seat just as our food arrives and begins gnawing on Alex's breadstick without missing a beat.

A dull laugh bounces through me. "Well, wasn't that the slap that was heard around the world. Let me guess. He's finally clued you in on his deviant bedroom preferences?"

Cormack is quick to avert her eyes. "As if anything of that nature could possibly scare me off. It was far worse than that. He suggested I pay for my own dinner."

It all makes perfect sense.

And now I realize how Noah could have gotten rid of her all along. Sure, it would have caused some mild bodily harm, but nothing like wrapping him around a tree while going over eighty miles an hour. It would be just my luck for Cormack to come out unscathed.

The least the universe could have done was split the injuries between the two. That way Noah might have had a fighting chance.

"Suzanna." Cormack glowers at the woman and Suze's entire body ignites in spontaneous flames—okay, so they're figurative, but they are there.

Suze leans in toward the blonde malfeasance that just landed among us, her eyes narrowed in like sharpened spears.

Noah moans, "Everett, be ready to act. I don't like where this is going."

In one quick move, Suze leans back and smiles our way, her lids shuttering like that of a defunct doll.

"Everett"—she begins—"I'd like to employ a restraining order against Cormack Featherby, and I'd like to procure one on behalf of my son as well. I need it in place by morning. And if you won't do it, I'll find someone who will."

Everett offers a disappointed glance to the two of them. "And I will get right on that."

"Wow," Noah muses. "I think Cormack is getting off easy. The last person who called my mother by her given name ended up with their dinner in their lap."

"I get it," I say to the older woman and her eyes dart to mine like a threat. "My name is actually Carlotta, but no one dares call me that. I go by the nickname my adoptive mother gave me, *Lottie*. So I understand the whole Suze/Suzanna thing. Was that your birth mother's name, too?"

All breathing seems to have ceased at the table. Noah gives an exasperated sigh on my behalf, most likely because he can't do a thing to aid in the situation.

And then, just like that, Suze's face softens a touch. She takes a deep breath and nods my way, and I think I may have finally broken through her frosty exterior.

"That is exactly what happened." She stands. "Now if you'll excuse me." She lands her hand over the lip of Cormack's plate—Alex's as it were—and sends pasta carbonara sailing over her chest.

Cormack howls as she bounces to her feet, shouting something about a Prada original followed by a string of expletives so salty I think we all lost ten IQ points listening to it.

"Carlotta." Suze quickly pulls the same stunt with my own plate, and I'm left wearing my warm, soggy dinner as she takes off in a huff.

I shrug over at Noah and Everett. "I guess she has a short fuse."

Gemma clip-clops her way over in a panic. "Oh, Lottie! You've been attacked!" She gasps at Cormack. "There's been a massacre!" she brays out the words. "Have you been shot? Stabbed?"

"I've been spaghettied," I say, standing up and the food slides right off of me. Everett stands along with me, our hands still conjoined while he does his best to mop up the mess for me.

"And the baby?" Gemma does an odd little panicked dance. "Is Everett's baby all right?"

Noah's mouth falls open, his eyes wide with surprise as he looks to Everett and me.

"Lottie, are you pregnant?" There's a touch of panic in his voice, and in no way do I want to panic Noah, but a stream of words is piling up in my throat all at once and I can't seem to get the truth out. "Oh my goodness, you are." He takes a staggering step back.

Gemma wobbles to and fro. "Oh dear, I don't think I was supposed to say that in front of Noah, was I?"

Noah closes his eyes a moment. "You don't have to hide anything from me, Lottie." His gaze shifts to his old stepbrother. "And neither do you, Everett. Congratulations to you both. I mean that." His body begins to dissipate, and he glances down at his hands as he evaporates to nothing.

"Noah, wait!" I call out after him. "Noah, please!"

Cormack huffs as she works to scrub the food off her dress. "You'd better get her home, Essex. The garlic has gone straight to her head."

More like a misconception has gone straight to Noah's heart.

I don't know what's worse at this point—Noah finding out the fact he's the father, or letting him believe that Everett is.

The only thing I do know is, things couldn't get any worse if they tried.

12

Horror.

That's exactly what this is.

I spend the next few days baking my fingers to the bone, trying to digest how it came to be that Noah found out I was with child—and alarmingly he thinks the child is Everett's. I don't blame Gemma. She came to the house that night, walked right through the front door, and planted herself in front of the fireplace, moaning and groaning for me to forgive her. Of course, I spent the better half of an hour doing just that and both Pancake and Waffles seemed amused by my efforts.

But because of this baby-induced debacle, I've spent more than my fair share of time at the hospital whispering *I love you* and *I need you* into Noah's ear.

I'm terrified he won't ever want to wake up. I'm downright afraid that Noah won't want to live in a world where Everett and I are having a child—especially while Noah and I are still legally married. He must think the worst of me. I can imagine this has all been a pretty big blow to his heart.

Everett has been equally concerned for Noah. He heads over to the hospital himself before picking up dinner and coming home. And just the thought of him spending so much time with his former stepbrother warms my heart and makes me love him that much more—something I'm sure Noah would roll his eyes at.

I get it. But I can't help it.

And those are the very reasons the bakery is in a serious surplus of pumpkin pies, pumpkin rolls, pumpkin cheesecake, pumpkin cinnamon rolls, pumpkin pinwheels, pumpkin scones, pumpkin glazed donuts, and even scrumptious pumpkin croissants this morning.

Lily moans as she takes a bite out of a fresh baked pumpkin cinnamon roll.

"I'm really sorry you're stressing out about Noah, but boy am I glad you're stressing out about Noah during pumpkin season. I've already gained fifteen pounds since walking through the door this morning."

"I'm glad you can benefit."

It's the middle of the afternoon, and as far as Lily is concerned, I'm stress baking because Noah doesn't seem to be waking up.

Little does she know that I'm stress baking because I'm afraid I've inadvertently finished him off. All because of one precious baby-sized secret. And that's exactly why I've decided not to tell another living soul about the baby.

Heaven knows if the deceased souls can't be trusted, the living souls are worse. I texted both Carlotta and Mayor Nash—aka bio daddy—and threatened them within an inch of their big-mouthed lives. Parricide is a very real phenomenon, and I'm guessing it's often brought about when the parents go about blabbing their child's most intimate DNA-riddled secrets to anyone who'll listen.

No—my sweet secret will have to remain tucked safely in my womb until I can tell Noah the truth myself. But I still haven't decided if the truth is better than the lie. The truth might be quicker to kill him if he realizes that Everett just might be raising his child. Or it might motivate him to fight harder to wake the heck up. But the pendulum swings too wide for me to fire off the news willy-nilly, so baking up a storm it is.

The door to the Cutie Pie Bakery and Cakery chimes and in walks Naomi Turner, eyes bulging, her face red with rage, honing all of her fury at her one-time best friend—in other words, it's just another Thursday. Her dark hair is slicked back into a ponytail, and she's bundled up in a green wool coat and matching scarf.

Just past her, those dark clouds pressing down over our sleepy town never seem to leave Honey Hollow anymore, and I wonder if it's a somber warning of some kind.

"Have I got a bone to pick with you." Naomi's voice shakes with rage, and I roll my eyes all the way up to those twinkle lights glistening in the café. More and more I find myself mesmerized by the branches of that oak that extend into the café from the Honey Pot Diner next door. And every time I'm delighted by looking at them and feel as if my grandmother, Nell Sawyer herself, just gave me a hug from the other side.

Lily slams shut the baked goods compartment that faces the customers and nearly shatters the glass in the process.

"You always have a bone to pick with me, Naomi. What now"—she leans in—"you cow."

I suck in a quick breath.

"Okay, girls, let's relegate the name calling, and the cat fighting, to the alley out back. I don't want you scaring off the customers. And don't think for a minute of using my bakery as a wrestling ring to work out your differences." Not that it hasn't been done before.

Naomi smirks. "I wouldn't dream of stooping to her level. I'm above the name-calling and the cat fighting. I was simply coming by to let Lily know that I have a little something of hers." She pulls a lacy pink ball from her purse and chucks it onto the counter. "Your underwear, I believe."

"Eww, gross!" I yelp so loud half the customers turn this way to gawk at the horror.

I grab a piece of wax paper and swat the pink panties onto the floor before getting right to the task of disinfecting the counter with a spray bottle I keep under the register for less than hygienic emergencies such as this. Not that I've had a pair of underwear on my counter before nor do I care to ever again.

Lily gasps as she swipes them off the floor and shoves them into her apron.

"Those are La Perla," she hisses. "Everyone knows you don't roll La Perla into a ball and toss them about!"

Naomi leans in. "Isn't that what you wanted Alex to do with them?"

Lily snorts. "That *is* what he did with them, but I liked his intentions a lot more than I like yours."

Naomi's nostrils flare the way Keelie's do just before she's about to blow. "I know all about your intentions, and they're not nearly as wholesome as you'd like for people to believe them to be. I was at his place last night when I stumbled upon those beauties tucked beneath his pillow."

Lily's lips twitch with a satisfactory smile. "Just where I left them. I hope they inspired him to have very naughty dreams about me."

I groan as a couple of older women quickly abandon their table and scuttle right out the door.

Naomi lets out a sharp bite of a laugh. "He couldn't be dreaming about you because I was there keeping him too busy to sleep."

Lily attempts to lunge over the counter and I hold up a hand, stopping her midflight.

"Lily"—I take a quick breath in the event I need to employ my own wrestling moves in a moment—"why don't you take a break? Maybe rinse your hands and apron with bleach or something? I'll make up a box for Naomi to take back to the staff at the Evergreen Manor because she was just leaving."

Naomi rolls her eyes, but Lily is quick to comply with my wishes.

"Are you crazy coming in here and confronting her like that?" I hiss as we watch Lily walk straight out the front door for some air. Lord knows there's not enough air in all of Honey Hollow to defuse that ball of anger.

Naomi shrugs. "She's the one that started it. I wasn't going to sleep with Alex at all until he settled his feelings for us. But Lily drew first play at his mattress and left me with no choice but to compete."

"Ugh. You're both doing it with him? That's beyond reprehensible. You were lifelong best friends before he came to town, and in five hot Alex Fox minutes, he inadvertently managed to dismantle what it took a lifetime for the two of you to build."

"Oh, relax. You've always been so dramatic. So he's taking us for a test drive, so what? We both secretly wanted it. And now that I've gotten a preview myself, I know exactly what I'm fighting for." She sets her hands down on the counter and leans hard on them as a faraway look takes over her eyes. "He's incredible, Lottie. If Noah was half as good as he is, I have no clue what you're still doing with that judge."

"Yes, well, don't forget I've done the deed with that legal eagle, too."

"And?" Her eyes bulge with the question.

"And it's none of your business. Do me a favor and keep your boyfriend squabble outside these doors. In fact"—I start while quickly putting together that box of goodies I promised—"why don't you head outside these doors and apologize to Lily for letting a boy, of all things, get between you? It goes strictly against girl code to behave this way. Only one of you will end up with Alex. Don't let him turn you into something you never wanted to be. No man is worth taking down a friendship." I slide the box of sweet pumpkin treats her way. "They're on me."

"Thank you," she says, quickly cradling it in her arms like a tiny pink bundle.

Hey? I wonder if Noah and I will have a boy or a girl?

"Lottie"—Naomi grunts as if she were under great compulsion to speak to me, and I have no doubt she is, considering the fact I'm far from her favorite person—"I just want to thank you for adding a little clarity to the situation for me. I was so bent on winning Alex—and I always win, we both know that—I actually lost sight of Lily. I guess it's time to rectify that."

"Naomi, that's great. So you're going to apologize to Lily for your behavior and the two of you are going to figure out the best way to deal with this situation?"

"Heck no. Lily will apologize to me, and then we'll head down to the Scarlet Sage Boutique together and she'll help me pick out my own La Perla panties. Because that's what best friends do."

"Yes, they pick out unmentionables to entertain their shared boyfriends with."

She turns to leave and a thought hits me. "Naomi? What's Trisha's old assistant doing now that she's sort of out of a job? Is she *your* new assistant?"

Her chest bounces at the idea. "I don't need an assistant. I have an entire staff already in place to help me. Trisha didn't need one either. I never understood how the company let that fly—especially Trisha. For someone who liked to point the finger at my *egregious* spending, she sure indulged in her own wasteful squandering of profits. Jade is no longer with the Evergreen."

"Do you know where she went?"

She crimps a wicked smile as she trots back close to the counter. "She wanted in with the Elite Entourage, but her own friend Annette Havershem wouldn't let her in." I make a face. Let's not forget Naomi herself was with the EE for a time.

"Where did she end up?"

"She's working the house—the Red Room Playhouse is Red Satin's dirty cousin."

"You mean it could get dirtier than Red Satin?"

She gives a single nod. "The Canelli brothers own both."

I gasp at the mention of their wicked name. The Canellis are a huge crime family that run Leeds and own just about every seedy part of it. I helped put their baby sister away for a very long time, so I'm betting they're not too happy with me right about now.

Meg works at Red Satin—that's the seedy establishment in which she teaches strippers to shimmy.

Naomi shrugs. "Jade is doing the bawdy story time for adults. It's basically the opening act before the girls come on stage. It's not quite a strip club like Red Satin. We're talking burlesque, dinner theater type stuff. It's just another venue the Elite Entourage uses to bring in customers. All the girls are encouraged to mingle after the show, and the men are typically great tippers. I used to haul in fifteen grand a month when I was doing it myself."

My eyes bulge the size of my pumpkin cinnamon rolls.

She shrugs again. "It's good work if you can get it. Easier than the glam dates the EE hooks you up with. I think that's why Annette put Jade there. She told me once she sees her as a little sister."

"What made you transfer from such a cushy gig to the mean streets of the EE dating scene?" And I use the term *dating* as loosely as their morals.

"They only let the new girls do that. It's sort of an indoctrination process. Get them used to the money, the glitz, and the glamour, and then throw them out to the wolves." Naomi deflates as if she just relived her poor choices in a microsecond.

"You're not still doing that, are you?" I ask with the utmost caution in the event she decides to fling the contents of that box my way.

"I was up until I met Alex. And now I only do group dates on nights he's with Lily. I guess you could say he's tamed my wild side. And before you let your filthy mind wander, I've never opted to take the date to home base. The girls always make the final call, and we always get paid for our time."

"Good for you, Naomi. I'd be lying if I said that didn't give me any relief. You deserve to be loved by a man."

"I suppose so. But earning a couple hundred dollars a date doesn't hurt either."

She takes off and I pull out my phone and text a certain judge that I love.

The Red Room Playhouse. Tonight. Are you up for some naughty story time?

Everett texts right back. **I'm always up for getting naughty with you.**

My lips twist as I read his response. Yes, Everett is always a willing participant in my schemes, and at one point I was a willing participant in his bedroom. I feel terrible he's put his body on ice just for me.

I wonder what Everett would do if I encouraged him to see other people?

A brief vision of an entire gaggle of woman dog-piling on top of him in a free-for-all flits through my mind, and I quickly flit it right back out. The thought of Everett with another woman brings my blood to an instant boil.

On second thought, I'm far too greedy to let Everett back into the wild.

Too bad I can't seem to give myself sound advice the way I so easily doled it out to Naomi. My heart is still very much spliced in half, and I've inadvertently gifted it to two different men. I'm not throwing Everett to the estrogen-based wolves, and I'm not giving Noah over to death either. I want them both right here by my side until it becomes crystal clear what I should do.

In the meantime, I'm going to visit with Jade Pope tonight, and hopefully it will become crystal clear who killed Trisha Maples.

Something has to give, and I'm hoping that something is Jade Pope's loose lips.

13

The Red Room Playhouse is a regal looking building that stands erect just a few paces down the street from Red Satin. The clientele looks remarkably world-class, nothing but distinguished men of every age dressed to impress the hookers in training. There's even a smattering of women sprinkled about, and even they look elegant and impeccable.

Everett looks downright alarming in his gray suit. His slick silver tie makes his blue eyes glow like homing beacons for any lady of the night worth her salt to migrate to. And, of course, I'm not impervious to his comely appearance.

"Everett, you don't play fair," I hiss as he takes up my hand and growls out a dull laugh. "You realize that we're in a no-fly zone and yet you look like this in my presence. I really need to find the shut-off valve for my attraction to you."

His lids lower just a notch until it looks as if he's smoldering at me. "Lemon, you just say the word and I'll help you with your needs. From what I've read, your needs will only increase as those hormones pour through you."

"And, believe me, they are. I've been running hot and cold from rage to—well, grief. Everett, since Noah landed in the hospital, it feels as if we've been on a never-ending roller coaster of emotion."

His eyes widen a notch at something behind me. "Prepare for another bumpy ride."

I turn around and gasp at the sight before me.

Striding this way, grinning from ear-to-ear, are both Carlotta and Mayor Nash.

"Oh my goodness," I moan as if I were about to be sick.

"Lottie Lemon." Carlotta slaps me on the back. "It's nice to see you stepping out for a good old-fashioned raunchy date night with the plus one stand-in."

I scoff. "Everett is no stand-in. We're—" Oh Lord, I have zero clue what Everett and I are.

Mayor Nash leans in with that grin still satiating his face. "You're parents. Or soon-to-be. Congratulations, Lottie. Judge Baxter. Of course, I won't tell a soul."

"Thank you." I scowl at Carlotta because I assume it will be asking a bit too much for her to agree to go along with his good sense—not that he has a history of good sense. It's well known Mayor Nash is a serial philanderer. "What are the two of you doing here?"

Carlotta does this squiggly thing with her eyes that I can't quite decode, but, if I had to guess, I'd think she just stumbled upon something too good to believe.

"You mean you don't know?" She cocks her head to the side with a look of curiosity.

"Of course, we know," I say, rolling my eyes at Everett. "This is a bawdy book reading much like those that take place in my innocent bakery in the name of literature. Everett and I just thought we'd stop by and—" I shrug over at him in hopes he'll finish my ridiculous sentence for me.

He nods. "And whet our appetite before we head home and get to bed. Having Noah in the hospital isn't exactly an aphrodisiac."

"Oh, good Lord. Et tu, Everett?"

Carlotta chortles up a storm. "I believe it's Essex to you, Lottie. And don't you worry. Your bawdy secret is safe with me. I won't breathe a word of any of this to your mother."

"Thank you, Carlotta. You have no idea how much this means to me."

The doors open, and soon the glut of men in suits, the smattering of well-dressed women, all file inside at record speed as if a wall of fire were pursuing them.

The interior of the playhouse looks every bit like an upscale theater, with its crimson-colored carpet and its glossy concession stand in the lobby. Three sets of double doors allow the masses to flood into the restaurant-style seating area. The small bistro tables each have a pumpkin dotting them along with a smoldering candle. The seats all quickly fill up, and Everett and I take a seat up front with Carlotta and Mayor Nash landing at the table next to us.

No, this isn't weird at all. I'm sure listening to Jade Pope read the dirty parts of a novel out loud in front of my biological parents won't traumatize me one bit.

The lights begin to dim and I lean in toward Everett.

"I think you had it wrong, Judge Baxter. In no way could listening to this stuff while seated a stone's throw from the woman who bore me act like an aphrodisiac. And Mayor Nash, too?" I whisper while pretending to gag.

Everett grunts as he tucks his lips to my ear. "Good thing I know a naughty story or two I can share once we're alone."

My stomach bisects with heat at the thought, and I offer a wry smile.

"Now that might work." Something says there will be no stopping him. "And I guess it could be worse." I shrug up at him. "My mother could be here."

The lights go out before a bunch of hot pink spotlights swirl around the room, and to my horror they shine right over the center of the stage to reveal a ten-foot tall llama with a buck-toothed grin.

"Can you see me, Lottie?" Gemma brays the words out, and I take up Everett's hand so he can hear her as well. "I'm having a tough time seeing you because the lights are so bright." She staggers from one end of the stage to the other just as Jade Pope jumps onto the platform and strides down to the end with her arms held high to the rhythm of a thunderous applause. I get the feeling they get a lot of repeat customers around here. Jade's dark hair is pulled back, and her skin has an alien-like glow. She's cute in a girl next-door kind of way with a boxy face and a smile that drifts from ear-to-ear.

Gemma looks stunned to see the brunette with her hair up in a glossy bun, outfitted in nothing more than a gold bustier with a matching underwear and a white long feathered boa draped around her shoulders.

"Oh, she's pretty, Lottie! More people should wear feathers, don't you think?"

Everett leans in. "I agree. How about I get you a boa for Christmas?"

I shoot him a look.

Jade Pope laughs into the microphone in her hand. "Good evening, ladies and gentlemen. Welcome to the Red Room Playhouse, where we are proud to host open mic night. This evening's lineup is a crop of writers who bring you their stories hot off the keyboard press. Let's give it up for our first guest of the night—a midnight mistress who writes under the pseudonym *Mirandy Lemonade*!"

"Oh my goodness." I don't believe my ears or my eyes as I spot my bouncy blonde mother jumping out on stage. She gives the audience a quick wave before scuttling next to Jade.

A couple of stagehands bring out two stools and swing over a microphone on a stand at a comfortable height for my mother.

"Oh no." My stomach explodes in a vat of acid at the prospect of what's about to ensue.

Mom leans into the mic and titters with laughter. "Good evening, fine people of the playhouse." Her voice is unusually low and guttural, and it's only then I note she's wearing garishly dark red lipstick. She's donned a fiery red dress for the evening, high neck, tea-length hemline, and a pair of black strappy heels that I'm pretty sure I've never seen on her feet before. She very much looks as if she's about to put on a show, and I very much look like I'm eyeing the exit.

She shields her eyes with her left hand while her right clutches at what looks to be a three-ring binder. She stops abruptly in her visual hunt once she spots Carlotta.

"Oh, I've got good friends supporting me here tonight, and my sweetheart, too." She waves to the corner where I spot that silver two-timing fox, Topper Blakley, waving while seated with a seedy blonde dripping off his side like Honey Hollow honey—Cormack. Heaven help us all. "And, of course"—my mother continues to open her volatile mouth—"I have all of you to help quell my nerves. You might say that you will get to see me step into another dimension of my being. I've never done this before. I guess it's kind of exciting to have all of you here to witness my very first time."

A round of catcalls and applause breaks out at my mother's unintentional, or perhaps intentional double entendre.

I'm not sure if I know *Mirandy Lemonade* like I thought I did.

Her eyes hook to mine, and something between a cry for help and the sound you make just before you vomit emits from her.

Believe me, the feeling is mutual.

Gemma chortles out a laugh as she hops down from the stage and sits at my feet. "Oh, this should be good, Lottie. I'm sure you've heard your mother tell quite a number of bedtime stories."

"Yes, but none like this," I mutter.

"Oh dear." Mom bats her hand my way. "I don't know if I can do this." She clears her throat into the mic. "My daughter is here," she snips it out in a fit of frustration as if to say I've gone and ruined everything.

The room fills with boos and hisses, and Jade takes a moment to scowl at me as well.

Great. There's nothing like having your overall presence decried by a crowd of horny onlookers.

Jade leans into the mic a moment. "Mirandy, it's entirely up to you if you wish to go on. Just know that you have an eager fan base at the ready, and I'm sure everyone in this room would love a copy of your book once it comes out."

Mom waves her off, her face turning a perky shade of pink as she giggles like a schoolgirl. The crowd begins to chant and cry out, encouraging her to *read the book, read the book.*

"Oh, all right." My mother bubbles with a laugh as she shrugs to her newfound fans. "Lottie, you'll have to forgive me. But there comes a time in every child's life that they need to recognize the fact that mothers are sexual beings."

Everett leans in. "No, they don't."

Mom winks my way. "In fact, a lot of these things I'm about to read out loud are a mixture of things that your father and I experienced in our most intimate moments."

"Kill me now."

Everett gives my hand a squeeze, and I'm hoping that's a sign he's willing to comply.

Mom lifts a finger in the air. "Full disclosure—there's a bit of every lover I've ever been with thrown into the mix. The title of my steamy read is *The Pastor Within.*"

Carlotta belts me on the arm as she leans in and whispers, "I bet this is a risqué exposé on that preacher you offed last month."

"Great." I can't wait to hear all about my mother's dalliances with that nutcase.

And hear it I do.

My mother goes into the grisly details, ad nauseam, for the better part of a half hour before Jade has to cut her off in order to fit in a couple more perverted guests. Soon enough, the showgirls come out and I'm right back to being blindsided as I see my very own sister—half-sister as it were—kicking her scantily clad legs with the best of them.

Kelleth Nash grins with that fuchsia painted on smile right up until the end, completely oblivious to the fact her father is in the room.

I suppose my father and I have finally found something to bond over—the fact we've seen way too much from the people we love.

I glance his way, only to find that Mayor Nash is suspiciously missing. My bet is he's in the bathroom losing his dinner.

The stage lights come back up, and Jade thanks the audience for being so wonderful—more like green around the gills if you count Mayor Nash and me.

The showgirls drift down into the audience and begin to mingle with the crowd, and I excuse myself from Everett as I make a beeline for that new sister of mine.

Kelleth is in the middle of closing a deal with what looks to be a balding big tipper just as I haul her off to the side. Her blonde hair is long and wild, and she's donned a bit more makeup than I'm accustomed to her wearing to the point where she hardly looks recognizable. Although, maybe that's the point.

I yank her well out of his horny midst. "What in the world are you thinking?"

"Would you let go?" Kelleth pulls away. "I wouldn't have to resort to dancing for tips if you hadn't had my fiancé arrested for racketeering."

I groan at the memory. "Okay, fine. This is all my fault. But for Pete's sake, find another means of employment."

Cormack crops up once again where she's not wanted. And how does she always keep doing this?

"Ignore her, Kelleth." Cormack does that weird air-kissing thing with my sister. "Laurie is always so ready to judge. But you can't blame her. The love of our lives is hanging by a thread." She shrugs it off as if it were no big deal. "Guess what?" She takes up my sister's hand. "Cressida is coming to town and she's going to stay with me at that bawdy B&B." She belts out a husky laugh, and Kelleth gasps as if she's just gotten the best news ever.

"Who's Cressida?" I ask as if I actually cared. Right now, I just want to maintain my position in the conversation.

Kelleth averts her eyes. "My old college roommate. The three of us have been friends since childhood."

Wow, Cormack knew my sisters way back when, and all the while she was dating both Everett and Noah? I guess there really are only six degrees of separation between just about everyone on this spinning blue marble. And with Cormack and me there seems to be less than three.

Cormack nods as if she heard. "I'm picking her up tomorrow and then we're doing lunch." She sneers my way.

"She'll be thrilled to know Essex is still in the vicinity, but she won't believe for a minute he's engaged."

"Oh?" I muse. "Is she an Essex groupie, too?" It wouldn't surprise me one bit. Everett bedded his way through all of Vermont before he met me.

Cormack's eyes do their best impression of my pinwheel cookies. "You mean to tell me that Essex hasn't told you about Cressida?"

First my mother, now this?

I shake my head at both of them. "No, and I don't want to know a thing about the woman." I lean in toward my sister. "Kelleth, you can do better than this. Oh, and your father is here."

Her mouth falls open as she quickly scans the vicinity before spotting him with my mother and Carlotta.

"Oh my goodness!" Kelleth howls and runs right out the nearest fire exit.

Before I can gasp or go after her like a good sister would, Gemma clip-clops her way over.

"Lottie, come quick! Our suspect is leaving."

I turn in the direction Gemma's long neck is pointed and spot Jade already dressed in her street clothes with a purse cinched over her shoulder as she makes her way to the bar. Her dark hair is up in a ponytail and her makeup has been wiped clean. She looks all of twelve and as adorable as can be. I do my best to thread my way through the crowd, only to cut her off at the pass before she makes it to the door.

"Jade!" I say breathlessly. "That was quite a show." I drum up a warm laugh as if we were old friends. "Do you think we can talk?"

Jade wrinkles her nose my way. Those cat eyes of hers glow a brilliant shade of green, and they make me want to bolt out the door and all the way to Honey Hollow General to visit Noah and tell him the truth about our baby.

"I'm sorry. I'm off for the rest of the night and I'm not into girls. You might try the women at the bar, though. I've heard stories."

"What?" I jump in front of her as she tries to make her way around me. "No, I'm not here for that. I was in the audience, and I wanted to say hello. Trisha introduced us the night of the charity event. The night—"

"She was killed!" Her face bleaches white with shock. "I'm sorry. It was such a crazy night. I don't really remember much from it."

"I baked the pies for the event. We were introduced that night. I'm Lottie Lemon."

"Oh"—her forehead wrinkles a moment—"that's right. You were there with Annette and Gerrie." She rolls her eyes. "And Lou." She shudders. "So, have they arrested him yet?"

My mouth falls open. "Annette said the very same thing."

A choking sound comes from her. "She never was the brightest bulb," she says under her breath before clearing her throat. "Up until now, that is. I tried telling her for months that Leo was pulling one over on Trisha. I told Trisha, too. I guess now that the smoke has cleared, and poor Trisha is dead, Annette finally sees the error of her ways." She glances out the door a moment. "Trisha didn't know a lot about the man that she believed would become her fiancé."

"Oh, I spoke to Leo. My mother—the tall glass of randy Lemonade you had the displeasure to listen to? We took a writing class with him at the library the other day. He just so happened to be the teacher. So, of course, I went up to him after class and we talked about poor Trisha. He said he had a ring to give her and everything. He said he gave it to her daughter instead as a keepsake. He figured Trisha would have wanted it that way."

A loud laugh pumps from her, and it catches me off guard.

"If you believe that, I've got some beachfront property to sell you in Ashford. What the good teacher failed to mention was that the ring was never meant for Trisha."

"But you said yourself they were about to get engaged."

She shakes her head. "Trisha knew he was shopping for a ring. What she didn't know was that he was having an affair with her daughter. Can you imagine? Carrying on with both of them like that? In my opinion, whoever killed Trisha should have been aiming for Leo and Chanelle instead. They're nothing but a couple of animals in my book. But then, Chanelle hated her mother so much she would have done anything to make her life miserable, including steal her man. I would have never done that to any member of my family—that is, if I still had a family."

I cringe inside because I can feel the words bubbling to the surface. "Jade, what happened to your family?"

"My parents died a long time ago. It was just my brother and me up until a few months ago and then I lost him, too. But don't feel sorry for me. I'm soldiering on." She gives a long blink. "I've got this place to keep me busy, and I'm looking to get my real estate license. Sometimes you just have to take what life gives you and make the best of it. Sort of like your mom. She said her tagline is *taking life's lusty lemons and making lemonade*."

"And, sadly, I can attest she's done just that."

A soft laugh bubbles from her. "It was nice talking to you, Lottie."

She takes off before I can ask another question.

I head back into the theater just as Carlotta and my mother are stepping out.

Mom wraps her arms around me. "Oh, Lottie! How did I do? At first, I didn't think I could do it at all with you in the audience. But once I understood that you came out just to lend your support, I knew I couldn't let you down. I just had to buck up and power through it."

"And power through it you did. That was quite descriptive stuff you were saying about Pastor *Maines*." She didn't do a whole lot to disguise his name. It's not a big leap from Gaines to Maines. "And you certainly didn't skirt around the bush in that steamy scene that took place in the parsonage."

Mom chortles with her fingers pressed to her lips. "Stop it, Lottie. You're making me blush just thinking about it."

Carlotta hacks out a laugh. "Face it, Mirandy. You're not capable of blushing. We'd better go. Harry dashed out the door once he heard his baby girl made a run for it." She slaps my mother on the back. "Hey? Maybe if we're lucky we can mow him down in the parking lot?"

Mom's shoulders jump as she laughs. "Now that does sound like fun," she says as the two of them head off to presumably run over the man who helped land me on this hot mess of a planet to begin with.

Now to find Everett and vacate the premises.

Gemma trots up, her neck jutting back and forth in a comical way, and I can't help but smile at her.

"Gemma, have you seen Everett?" It's so crowded in here and the music is still blaring from the speakers, I doubt anyone will care if I'm talking to myself.

"I'm sorry, dear. That savage looking beast in the corner waylaid me for a moment. I tried my best to get his attention but to no avail."

"What beast?" I crane my neck, only to find a set of oversized speakers in the corner with a fuzzy throw over them. "Gemma, that's a blanket."

She takes a step back and peers that way. "No, not that. The other corner."

I look in the other direction and gasp. Next to the wall stands a stuffed white bear with his fangs dripping to a sharpened point.

Lovely. Makes total sense.

"Don't worry, Gemma. He doesn't know what he's missing with you. Besides, would you look at all those girls congregating around him?"

And then it hits me. Those girls aren't clustering around that ferocious beast. They're off to the right just a notch, and I bet that's exactly where I'll find another sexy beast, the one that belongs to me—sort of.

I excuse myself and speed in that direction.

Sure enough, I spot a dark head of hair, and I quickly pluck Everett out of that boil of estrogen, out of the Red Room Playhouse, and straight for the parking lot.

"Lemon." Everett wraps his arms around me just before we get into the car. "Did you find anything out?"

"I found everything out—maybe." I reach up and give the stubble on his cheeks a quick scratch. "I also found out that you're still quite irresistible to the masses. But then, I already knew that."

A low rumbling goes off in his chest. "I'm not interested in the masses. I'm interested in one woman in particular." He bows in and gives my lips a chaste kiss. "Now let's get you home and get those feet up. It's hot cider for you and a cold shower for me."

I give a sad sigh at the thought. "Look at us. I'm knocked up, Noah is all but dead, and you're miserable."

His lips curl at the tips. "It will all work out, Lemon. I promise you that. How about we talk about the case on the way home? That should get our minds off our troubles."

"You always have a great solution for things. I think I'm going to keep you around."

"You couldn't get rid of me if you tried."

We talk about the case all the way home. I don't bring up that woman Cormack and Kelleth were talking about. Crescendo? Chrysanthemum? Oh, who cares.

Everett says that I couldn't get rid of him if I tried. But what if this Chrysolite person tried?

I don't want to even think about that.

Instead, I immerse myself in trying to pin down a killer.

Leo Workman and Chanelle Maples are starting to look pretty guilty.

How could Leo have been seeing both mother and daughter? He's perfectly vile for even entertaining it.

And how could Chanelle have murdered her own mother? That would be terrible if it were true.

What a big mess.

And murder is typically very, very messy.

14

Fall in Honey Hollow is usually never so cold, never so dark, never so heartbreakingly dismal.

It's late afternoon, just a few days after my poor ears were traumatized from listening to my mother talk about her psychotic ex and something to do with a riding crop—when Hook called asking both Everett and me to come down to his office to sign documents regarding the Maple Meadows Lodge in Hollyhock.

We're just about to pull into the parking lot of Redwood Realty when I get a spastic text from my ex, Bear, to meet him at the Diamond Stop, a jewelry store just down the street. Nothing he said made sense, so Everett and I head on over to meet up with him in the event he's gone and swallowed a ring and is awaiting his impending arrest. I'm pretty sure if that happened, they'd park Bear's hairy behind on the nearest potty and wait patiently until he produced that hunk of pressed carbon once again.

The Diamond Stop is a rectangular building with a giant glass jewelry counter that takes up the center of the room. Men and women dressed in formal wear work their magic behind the counter to make as many sales as possible just as Everett and I spot a woman in a red off the shoulder satin dress working Bear over and making him sweat.

"Lottie!" Bear practically jumps at the sight of me. His sandy blond hair is frazzled, and his face is red as a beet. He's got on a dirty sweatshirt that reads *Fisher Construction* across the front and he's paired it with a dusty pair of worn-out jeans. I can tell he came over in the middle of a job. "You gotta help me out. I thought I'd walk in and buy a ring. You know, a five-minute deal, but there are way too many choices. Who knew diamonds came in so many sizes?"

"Me," Everett says while looking at the array of glittery splendor underneath the glass cases.

I look to Everett questioningly but don't say a word. His wealthy upbringing most likely afforded him all the lessons he cared to learn on fine jewelry. Not long ago I was wearing his mother's shimmering rock on my left hand. Both his mother and sister still believe we're engaged. It's a little white lie Everett propagated before we ever met, and I just so happened to fill the mysterious future *Mrs.* shoes.

"Look"—Bear's eyes are bloodshot as if he's seen his last diamond—"I know that Keelie said we weren't going to do an engagement ring because she thinks it's redundant, but I want to give her a token of my appreciation. I've got a concrete mixer showing up in ten minutes at a job across town. You know what kind of jewelry Keelie likes better than I do. Why don't you pick out about five that you think she'd be really happy with and I'll stop by after work and pick one of those out? At least that way I won't be making a mistake."

"Yeah, sure, no problem. I know exactly what Keelie likes because we have the same taste." I lift my brows. "We both dated you, didn't we?"

Bear laughs and gives me a quick pat on the back. "And she's still going strong. I'll catch you both later. Oh, and Everett, I'm doing the property inspection of that lodge in Hollyhock for you tomorrow. I'll let you know if I find anything big." He takes off and I look to Everett.

"You have Bear looking at the property?"

"Along with a building inspector. I figure it couldn't hurt to get an extra opinion."

"Wise move. And I'm glad you believe in extra opinions because I'd love your opinion picking out these rings."

The brunette in the glowing red gown perks to life. "Are the two of you recently engaged?"

"We are," Everett pipes up with a manufactured grin. It's so rare to see a smile from this man, I soak it in and it warms me right down to my toes.

The woman's features smooth out. "Let's see your ring." She has a heart-shaped face and half-moon-shaped eyes and has an adorably tiny voice that emits from her.

"We don't have one," I confess.

"Yet," Everett corrects.

Her eyes light up with dollar signs. "Well, you just so happen to be in the right place. My name is Minerva, and I'll be glad to navigate you through the madness."

And navigate she does.

Everett and I walk the entire circumference of that giant glass case, and soon enough we have a dozen or so rings amassed between us.

Minerva lays them out, and one by one while I try them all on, I hold my hand out to admire them as I go.

Minerva leans in. "Everett, you have exquisite taste."

He presses those baby blues my way, a prickling of a smile on his lips. "I do, don't I?"

Minerva bubbles with a laugh. "Oh yes, in both women and diamonds. Lottie, I think you should choose one for Keelie *and* yourself."

Everett tips his head my way. "I think she's right."

"That's very kind of you, Everett, but I think I'll stick to Keelie's ring for now." I choose five different rings, all of which Everett selected. The man really knows what he's doing.

Everett puts his finger on the princess cut diamond encrusted with smaller stones.

"I chose this one for you, Lemon."

My entire body flushes with heat as he says it.

"Perfection!" Minerva trills. "A double cushion halo setting surrounded with round, brilliant cut diamonds."

"Everett"—I wrap my arms around him as Minerva gets to the task of putting the rings back in their proper places, sans the one that Everett has his eye on—"I love the ring, and I love you." My chest bucks with emotion just as his chest depresses with a sigh.

"I know, Lemon. Don't worry about it." He lands a gentle kiss to my cheek. "We have plenty of time to think about everything."

We wrap it up at the Diamond Stop and head back down the street until we end up inside Hook Redwood's office.

"Just sign here. We should get loan docs in a week, and then we're on track to getting the two of you the keys." Hook has his dark hair slicked back. He has a strong jaw and commanding eyes and a general likability about him. And most importantly, he treats Meg well and I truly appreciate that about him.

"It's all moving so fast," I say as I sign my life away.

"What's moving fast?" a female voice blurts it out curtly from behind, and I happen to recognize that curt voice as my own semi-sweet sister, Meg.

"Meg!" I jump up and pull her into a hug and she watches as Everett and I finish up. "Are you two up for lunch?" I don't mind one bit inviting them out for a bite with Everett and me.

Meg shakes her head out of the bun it's wound up in and a dark cascade falls over her shoulder. Every now and again I can see a glimmer of Lainey in her features, and because Lainey and I look so much alike, despite the fact I was adopted, I'd like to think that's a piece of me I'm seeing in there, too.

"Hook and I are headed out to the Ashford Hideaway just down the street."

The Ashford Hideaway is a quaint little motel that reminds me a bit of the lodge up in Hollyhock.

My entire body perks with surprise. "Are the two of you thinking of buying it?"

Meg belts out a laugh. "No, Lot. We're doing what normal people do at a hotel—we're getting a room. Hook doesn't have to be back until three."

"Oh." I bounce my brows at Everett.

Hook clears his desk in haste. "What are the two of you up to?"

Everett takes a breath. "We're heading to the Ashford Sheriff's Department and I'm turning her in. And then I thought I'd hunt down the next person on the suspect list and capture Trisha Maples' killer myself."

"Very funny, Judge Baxter," I say, pressing my shoulder to his.

Meg slaps her knee.

"He's turning you in, Lot. You'd better watch your back with this one." She's laughing so hard, she can't breathe. "Who's your next victim anyway?"

I make a face at her. "Chanelle Maples, and I don't have a clue where to find her."

"I do." Meg shakes her head. "Chanelle is one of my girls. And she's one of the best. She really knows how to shake what her mama gave her. But she doesn't work at Red Satin. She works at Posh down the street."

Hook moans as if he's familiar. "Posh is Red Satin's wealthy cousin. You'll need to fork it out for the cover and bring lots of bills for tips." He nods to Everett as if he were giving him direct orders. "The girls don't like cheapskates, and they make sure the bouncers know about it."

Meg folds her arms across her chest. "She's on tonight. Why don't the four of us head out for a double date? Meet us there at ten."

"*Ten*?" both Everett and I say in unison. We've been strictly adhering to an early bedtime because Everett is convinced my body needs all the rest it can get—and I'm convinced he likes holding me long into the night. That happens to be my favorite part of going to bed early, too.

"Yes." Meg nods at the two of us as if we had the nerve to ask. "She's got primo moves that she honed with yours truly. I like to check up on my students now and again, so she won't suspect a thing."

"That's great." I shake my head at Everett. "This is too good of an opportunity to pass up."

Everett's gaze drops to my belly, and I can feel his gaze warming my midsection. Everett loves this baby as much as I do, and it melts me just thinking about it.

"Fine. But we should ask Margo to open the bakery for you. I don't want you taxing yourself too much."

Margo is one of the five-star chefs that runs the kitchen at the Honey Pot Diner. She's opened for me before on a handful of occasions, and truly only she or her partner Mannford can be trusted with the task.

Meg bucks with a laugh. "She's got you wrapped around her little finger, doesn't she, Judge Baxter?" Meg pats me on the back. "Good work, Lot. Now if any of us run into trouble with the law, we'll know you've got a legal eagle on lockdown. See you turkeys at ten." She and Hook take off for their afternoon delight.

"She's right." Everett's cheek flinches. "You've got me wrapped around your little finger."

I pull him into a tight embrace. "And you are wrapped around me completely. I'm not just being literal. Next stop?"

"Ethel."

Everett drives us down to the Ashford Country Sheriff's Department just the way he promised, and my heart demands to explode from angst as we walk solemnly past Noah's office. The door is covered with sticky notes and messages from well-wishers right here in the precinct sending him get well messages, and my spirit soars at the thought of so many people rooting for him. I crack the door open and peer inside, and if I'm not mistaken, it still holds the faint scent of his cologne.

"Lemon"—Everett whispers warm into my ear—"we can visit him afterwards if you like." I nod. Tears blur my vision as Everett navigates us over to Ivy's desk and she quickly produces my long-lost friend, Ethel. The words *Glock 26 Gen4* are printed over her side and she looks just as dangerously stunning as I remember.

"Lottie—" Ivy tips her head back at the sight of me. She has her red hair in a chignon. It's pulled so tight her face is stretched back. It fits her rather tight and stuffy personality. "I suppose I don't have to warn you again to stay out of my investigation. I've questioned three suspects, and they all claim to have had an encounter with you."

I suck in a quick breath. "Are you asking them about me?"

Her lids hood low with what looks like fury. "I had to. I had a hunch you'd be snooping."

"Are you kidding me? You're putting me in danger. What if one of them is the killer and *they* think I'm snooping?"

She postures a moment. "Funny you should mention that. They all brought up the fact they thought you were snooping."

"At least tell me who *they* are."

"You know who they are. Annette Havershem, Leo Workman, and Jade Pope."

"Well then, it sounds as if you're one step behind me, Ivy." I can't help but smirk.

"And it sounds like you're one step from landing in handcuffs. You know—those shiny silver things I'm sure Judge Baxter has landed you in a time or two."

My face heats fifty shades of crimson as Everett's chest bounces with a dry laugh.

"Don't you dare laugh," I threaten as I tuck Ethel safely into my purse.

"How is Noah?" She looks to the two of us. "Or have you forgotten him already?"

"You wish," I say. I know she's teasing, but I can dish it out as good as she can. "He's the same for now, but I have news I can hardly wait to share with him. I'm certain it will give him that extra boost to push through this."

Okay, so I'm not certain, but I do like the idea of coming across as certain around Ivy.

"News?" Her lips pull tight as she openly mocks me. "You're leaving him for Everett and he's finally free to be with that blonde twit that won't leave him alone?"

I can't help but frown at her. "I'd laugh if it were funny. We'll see you later, Ivy."

"Stay away from the case, Lottie. I have a very bad feeling about this one, and my bad feelings are never wrong."

I avert my eyes a moment. "I'll do my best."

"Your best has landed you in hot water a time or two. Everett, talk some sense into her before she gets herself killed. If she keeps walking into danger, one of these days she won't be able to walk out."

Everett searches the room a moment as if processing this bit of dire news.

"Don't worry about me, Ivy," I say, taking up Everett's hand and leading him out the door. "I'll be just fine."

Everett and I get back into his car, and he pauses before starting up the engine.

"She's right, Lemon. You could get yourself killed—and it's not just you anymore."

My hand rides over my tummy, and I bite down hard on my lower lip. The thought of jeopardizing my child—*Noah's* child makes me sick to my stomach.

Everett lands his hand gently over mine. "I care about you both. I think maybe it's time to hang up the detective hat for a while—maybe forever. You're a mother now. You have everything to live for."

"You're right." A heavy feeling presses over me. "I will hang it up. Right after I talk to Chanelle."

Everett gives a wistful shake of the head and drives us back to Honey Hollow.

Could I really hang up a hat I've worn so consistently these last few months? It certainly doesn't feel like I can.

One thing I know for sure. I'm headed to Leeds tonight, and I'm going to watch one of Meg's best students shake what her mama gave her.

And it just so happens that her mama is dead.

Could she have been the one who pulled the trigger?

I'm about to find out.

15

There is something to be said for freezing your tushie off in the name of an investigation. Everett hustles me inside of the glossy black building that looks far too cosmopolitan to be located anywhere near downtown Leeds.

Posh is exactly as its name purports. It boasts of onyx hardwood flooring, mirrors everywhere you look—which give the place the illusion of being much larger than it is—smoky gray chandeliers hung from the ceilings, and the tables are small white marble beauties surrounded with burgundy quilted circular sofas.

It is indeed *posh* inside, and I'm not too sorry about it. The last place I want to be at this hour is someplace that looks as seedy as it sounds.

The music is twanging away through speakers as Meg leads us to a table up front and we watch a few girls do a tasteful little number while thankfully keeping their stitches right where they belong. I'm more than relieved to learn that this isn't exactly your run-of-the-mill strip joint. Instead, we're met with a classier version, with far more teasing going on and a lot less strip.

I had a moment of hesitation before we walked in tonight, and if it wasn't so icy out there, I would have turned right back around. Technically, I've brought my unborn child into a strip club, and for some reason—obvious reasons—that doesn't quite sit well with me.

It's not hard to envision a miniature version of Noah in my tummy—a little baby boy trying desperately to catch a glimpse of the salacious activity outside the womb while giving me a thumbs-up for taking him to his first strip club while in utero.

No, thank you.

A trio of blondes belly up to the stage, tossing dollar bills in the air as if they were as plentiful as toilet paper, screaming their heads off as if they were having the time of their lives.

"Hey!" Meg barks. "Sit down, girls. This isn't that kind of club."

The tallest of the three turns our way, and both Meg and I groan hard.

"Loddie?" Cormack Featherby herds her crew in our direction, and soon we're faced with Cormack and two dazzling blondes that look as if they could be in the running for Miss Universe.

"Essex?" The adorable one with a perfect pout and large doe eyes lets out a harrowing squeal and he pops right out of his seat—most likely in fright.

"Cressida Bentley?"

Oh Lord, it's Cressida. *That* Cressida whoever she is. The one Kelleth and Cormack were discussing, the one with a history with *my* man.

A twinge of guilt washes over me when I say that last part. I can't lay ownership of anyone, let alone a grown man—two of them if I'm being completely honest. But in the back of my mind my greedy self-conscious is screaming *why not?*

The girl dives over Everett as if he just saved her from a drowning ship, and the girl next to her offers the rest of us a meager wave.

"Larson Rosenberg?" Hook stands, looking pleasantly dazed, and soon enough the blonde is latched to his waist in the exact same manner that Cressida seems to be climbing Mount Baxter.

Meg growls, "Let's jump 'em on three, Lot. Don't be afraid to crash a chair over their bleached heads if need be. We don't have any refs watching, so everything goes."

Cormack is quick to pluck her friends loose lest they perish. I think she's been around long enough to know that Meg doesn't make empty threats.

Cressida looks like such a dainty girl, about my age, perhaps a smidge older, filling in the age gap between

Everett and me. Her eyes have that translucent appeal to them, and she has a pert little upturned nose.

"How rude of me." She over enunciates every word as she looks to the rest of us. "Essex was my first true love, and I'd like to think I was the same for him."

Cormack waves her off. "Go ahead, Essex. I'm a taken woman. You can tell the truth. Which one of us did you really give your heart to?"

Everett's lips curl at the thought. "You both bruised me good, but I saved my heart to give to this woman right here." He picks up my hand and kisses the back of it.

Cressida sucks in a hard breath as if she just discovered a bloody finger in her drink.

"*Her*?" It comes out accusatory and judgmental and not one bit kind whatsoever. "Essex! You've gone and gotten yourself a house frau." She inspects me from head to foot as if she might be sick.

Everett's chest bounces with a laugh, and I playfully, not so playfully, smack him on the arm.

"I'm Lottie Lemon, Everett's fiancée." I shrug because it's true at times like these.

"*Oh.*" Cressida manages to break that monosyllable word into four distinct pieces. "That's something we can work with." She gives Everett a hard wink. "I've been engaged a time or twenty-two myself."

The girl next to her looks just as obnoxiously beautiful, and there's an air of money around her only the truly wealthy seem to acquire.

"Larson Rosenberg. I dated Hook way back when." She growls out every word while looking right at him. And just as I would have suspected, Meg is growling right back. "Essex went to school with us for a time." She takes a moment to grimace at him. "I hope you've wiped that unfortunate episode that led up to graduation right out of your dirty mind." She gives a husky laugh. "But we shan't talk about that tonight."

No, we shan't, I want to say. And for Pete's sake, I wish everyone would stop calling my boyfriend Essex. Well—he is a boy who's a friend—oh hell, he's my boyfriend. I've got two. It's not the biggest crime, and certainly not the worst.

The music shifts to something moodier, and Meg barks at the girls to take a seat. "This is her song, Lot. I've worked on this routine with her for so long I can do it in my sleep."

Hook leans over. "Is that what those kicks are about in the middle of the night?"

"No," Meg grunts. "That's me telling you to stay on your side of the bed."

The lights dim a notch and a sprinkling of stars appears on stage, slowly filling out into a supernatural form, and for a moment I'm hopeful it's Noah. I wouldn't mind at all if he wanted to dance with a glorified stripper. I just need to speak to him again in the very worst way.

But it's not Noah. It's Gemma, filling out in her celestial glory. Gemma shines like the sun as she sways back and forth to the rhythm of the music. And I take up Everett's hand in the event she inevitably has something to say.

"Lottie Lemon!" She laughs as she hits one edge of the stage before staggering to the other side. "I think I've found my calling. You know they used to play music in the corral now and again, and I'd really get my groove on. I don't know why humans don't seem to understand that animals enjoy a good beat to boogie to ourselves. In fact, we might get along better if we cut a hayfield together a time or two."

Everett leans in. "This is the first time I'd love to see what you see, Lemon."

"Oh, it's a sight," I say with a laugh in my throat. "Gemma really knows what she's doing."

Meg leans back. "It's Moxy. That's Chanelle's stage name, not Gemma."

And sure enough, Chanelle, aka Moxy, bursts onto the stage with her red hair whipping back and forth and a pair of three-inch long lashes adhered to her eyes—each one covered in glitter. She's donned a simple black dress with a neckline that plunges down to her belly button and does a rather intimate looking dance with a chair that a stagehand just hoisted up there for her. Chanelle gives the room a lustful look as she sways and kicks and ends up doing the splits both ways before bouncing back up to her feet.

"Wow!" Cormack shouts and whistles with approval, as do Cressida and Larson.

Cormack runs up and tosses an entire fistful of dollars into the air, and we watch as they flutter down to the stage as delicate as butterflies.

Do you know what's not so delicate?

An entire herd of upscale strippers trampling the stage and diving for Cormack's green as if it were a free-for-all. They sweep the stage clean like a band of three-year-olds at the base of a headless piñata.

Meg whacks me on the arm. "What'd you think?"

"Whoa." Everett pulls me in protectively. "Watch your left hook, would you? Lottie is in a delicate state."

All eyes look my way as I give Everett's hand a death threat of a squeeze.

He leans in and whispers, "Sorry. I couldn't help it."

"He's right," I say. "I felt a cold coming on this morning. I think I just need some rest. In fact, I'm having Margo open up the bakery for me tomorrow so I can sleep in."

Hook nods as if it were understandable, but Meg is busy giving both Everett and me the stink eye.

Cressida takes up Everett's free hand. "So tell me, Essex." She runs her finger seductively along the inside of his wrist. "What's a girl have to do around here to get a tour of your chambers?" A husky growl brews in her throat and gives away her true intentions.

"Same." Larson sharpens her eyes over at Hook. She's petite and blonde, and looks about as sturdy as blown glass. Basically, she's everything Meg isn't. "I just got my real estate license." She gives Hook a barely-there wink. "Know of any good real estate offices that might be hiring agents?"

Hook's jaw unhinges. "What a coincidence. I happen to have a few openings right now at my Ashford office."

Meg spikes the heel of her stiletto through the top of his shoe and Hook groans as if she shot him.

"He means Fallbrook," my sister is quick to correct. "You could have the eastern part of the state. Hook and I have the west."

Larson makes a face at my sister, and now I'm fearing for her pretty blonde hair. Meg has always been a notorious hair-puller. Both Lainey and I can attest to that.

Hook looks like he's about to burst from holding back the pain my sister just inflicted.

I hope he considers that a fair warning.

"Swing by the Fallbrook office sometime." He shoots Meg the side-eye and my sister's shoulders sag.

"No, he's right," Meg says with a twinge of defeat. "It's the Ashford office that's hiring. Go ahead and stop by, you little strumpet. But just know that Hook is one hot property that's no longer on the market. I've staked my claim and you best not be knocking around on my front door. I let my fists fly first and then ask questions."

Goodness. If that doesn't scare her off, nothing will.

I look to Cressida whose fingers are now crawling up and down Everett's sleeve.

"What she said," I growl at the tall twerp. "But double for me. I answer the door with both arms swinging."

Before Cressida can object, or agree if she's wise, Chanelle comes bouncing and screaming this way and she and Meg get lost in some sorority girl-like reunion.

Meg turns our way. "Everyone, this is my best student in the whole wide world, Moxy Lady!" She holds her hands out at her as if she were presenting a prize, and Chanelle does a little spin with the honor.

Meg hitches her head for me to follow them as they head off to an alcove a few feet away.

"Mox, this is my sister, Lottie. She doesn't believe that I actually teach artists such as yourself for a living. She thinks I'm secretly working an espresso machine at the latte place down the street."

Chanelle is quick to brush it off with a laugh, exposing two perfect rows of teeth. She looks vaguely familiar, and yet I can't seem to place her.

"Well, I can assure you, Meg here isn't just another dance instructor. She's the cream of the crop." She's quick to sing my sister's praises. "Las Vegas lost out on this one and all of Vermont is reaping the benefits."

"That was quite an impressive routine," I say.

Speaking of which, Gemma stops midway through a rather bottom thumping move and glides on over as if she were too tired to clip-clop any longer.

"Oh, it's not Chanelle, is it?" Gemma looks more than disappointed to see her. "I remember when she was just a wee babe, Trisha used to bring her around. However, Trisha did love the bottle back then. I'm afraid she wasn't the best mother to the poor girl."

Bottle? I look to Chanelle with new eyes.

Bottle!

"That's where I remember you from," I say out loud and cover my mouth with my hand as an apology for the outburst. "You were at the Evergreen for the charity event."

Her eyes grow wide. "Meg, would you mind getting me some ice water? I can feel a leg cramp coming on."

"No problem." Meg does a disappearing act, and Chanelle's demeanor changes on a dime.

Chanelle walks me deeper into the alcove, and the garish sound of the music dampens quickly.

"If you don't mind, I'd rather no one know that I was at the Evergreen. My mother was actually murdered that night, and the last thing I want is that nosy detective trying to pin the horror on me."

Ivy is rather nosy, but only because it's her job.

"I won't say a word." Little does she know I'm far nosier than Ivy could ever hope to be. "I'm so sorry about your mother. Did you happen to see her that night before she was killed?"

She shakes her head. "It wasn't even her that I was there to see. My boyfriend was roaming the grounds, and I wanted to surprise him. My mother and I hadn't spoken in quite some time. She wasn't a good person for me to be around. In fact, she's the reason I ended up inside of a bottle for so many years."

"That's terrible. That must make things worse."

"Not really." She shrugs. "In a way I was prepared for it. My psychologist had me slowly cutting her out of my life. He called her a toxic person and he was right."

"And what does your boyfriend think of this?"

She flashes her left hand and a large diamond ring sparkles in the dim light.

Gemma gasps. "She's stolen him, Lottie. She's gone and taken the ring that Leo was about to give Trisha. But he wasn't going to give it to her, now was he? I think we've got our killer, Lottie. Arrest both of them."

I crimp a smile to the not-so subtle spook. She could be onto something.

"That's a gorgeous ring," I say to Chanelle. "I guess it's your fiancé then, right?"

"That's right. Oddly enough, he proposed the night my mother died. I guess that's the way the universe wanted it." She shrugs it off as if it were so.

The very same night?

"Do you have any idea who would want to see your mother dead?"

"Not a single clue." Her eyes flit to the stage as if maybe she did—as if maybe she were the biggest clue of them all. "But I'm not exactly chasing whoever did this either."

"Did you know anyone who was close to your mother? Gerrie Havershem?"

"Gerrie?" She inches back. "That's the hag from the shelter, right?"

I give an eager nod. Gerrie is next on my list.

"I don't know. But I do know her niece, Nettie. She's the pretty brunette who was tagging along with her aunt that night. I happened to catch up with her, and that's when I saw my mom. I saw my mother in a heated argument after I hit the bar. And instead of intervening, I sat it out and caught up with Nettie. And believe me, Nettie is all bark and no bite. There's no way she'd be angry enough at anyone to pull the trigger, let alone some woman nearly twice her age."

"Maybe your mother did something to enrage her aunt and she wanted to get back at her?"

"I wouldn't doubt that my mother enraged anyone. Enraging people was pretty much her forte."

"And what about your mother's boyfriend? The mystery writer? Leo?" I wince as I say his name, but I plan on pretending that I don't know her new fiancé and the mystery writer her mother was dating are one and the same.

"Leo?" She gives a few contrived blinks as she looks around. "I'm not entirely sure who you're talking about."

Fine. Have it your way.

"How about your mother's assistant? Jade Pope? I hear she lost her position with the Evergreen and is reading naughty stories at the Red Room Playhouse."

Chanelle bucks with a laugh. "That serves her right. Okay, not really." She pats the tears from her eyes with her pinkies. "Jade is a good girl. I knew both Jade and Annette growing up. Jade is more than familiar with death and dying. She took her parents' death pretty hard, but her brother helped her push through it. That boy was her rock. I suppose they're clinging hard to one another still. No matter what, Jade has Robby to help her out."

"Oh, I think I heard that her brother recently passed away."

Gemma brays, "You're good, Lottie. But I'm betting she's better at manipulation than you'll ever be."

Chanelle groans as if she were mourning him on the spot. "Not Robby! I bet Annette is devastated, too. She was pretty close to the two of them for a while. I'm surprised she didn't mention it. But then the deputies busted up the party that night, so she may not have had the chance."

"It does sound tragic."

Meg comes back with a couple of drinks.

"It was nice meeting you, Chanelle," I say. "Again, I'm sorry about your mother."

"Don't be." She takes a quick swig from the drink Meg just shoved her way. "I guess it was her time. Onward and forward." She lifts her drink as if proposing a toast and a mean shiver rides up my spine.

Gemma brays hard right in Chanelle's face and the girl makes a face.

"Why does it suddenly smell like a barn in here?"

I head back to the table and peel Cressida off Everett.

Cressida makes a face at me. "You're no fun." She scowls my way before turning back to Everett. "At least I got a chance to wish you a happy birthday in person." She dots a kiss to his cheek and I'm horrified, but it has nothing to do with that tiny smooch.

"Everett Essex Baxter." I pull him my way and look straight into those cobalt eyes. "How dare you forget to mention the fact it's your birthday. It's perfectly criminal, and I feel like a monster." Come to think of it, Everett did tell me months ago that his birthday was in November, but he didn't say when and I sort of forgot to pry further. "I'm the lousiest girlfriend on the planet."

A husky laugh rumbles through his chest. "Don't feel bad. I forgot myself." He wraps his arms around me tight.

"No, you didn't. You're just trying to make me feel better."

"Okay, so my mother and sister might have reminded me this morning, and the cake they had for me at work sealed the deal. But fret not. It was nowhere near the league of your confections. Not only do I have eyes for just one woman, but her cakes are the only ones for me as well."

I offer up a wry smile. "I'm throwing you a party. A big, obnoxious party with a cake big enough for me to jump out of."

He shakes his head emphatically. "I'm afraid I can't attend. I'll be too busy seated in front of your fireplace rubbing your feet."

"It sounds like I won't be attending either."

Everett shakes his head. "Tonight was more than enough."

"Good thing for you, tonight isn't over by a long shot."

Everett and I head back to Honey Hollow, and I make him stop by the bakery and pick a cake out of the display case. I quickly pipe on a secret message that I don't dare let him see until we're back at my place.

Everett pulls the lid back on the pink box that houses his double chocolate chiffon cake and looks at the words I've written for him.

"Happy birthday, Mr. Sexy. I love you," he growls the words out just as, well, *sexy* as can be. "Lemon"—he pulls me in and looks lovingly into my eyes—"that's about the nicest thing anyone has done for me. Thank you for that."

"Everett"—my eyes fill with tears—"you have been so kind to me. And the generosity you've shown me over the last few weeks has blown me away. I can never repay you. Happy birthday. I have a tiny gift for you." I shrug up at him.

His brows depress. “No gifts.”

I nod in a fit of rebellion as I hike up on my tiptoes and I offer up a single chaste kiss to his lips. I hold there for a few good seconds and feel the tension in him as if he were about to devour me. I pull back and we both take a deep breath.

His lips twitch with the hint of smile. “You give great gifts, Lemon.” He hitches his head toward the hall. “Now let’s make all my birthday wishes come true and have cake in bed.”

And we do just that.

It does feel nice like this with Everett.

And I feel guilty as heck about it, too.

It’s time to tell Noah about the baby. And if Noah won’t come to me, I’ll have to go to the hospital and whisper it into his ear and hope that he can hear me.

If only he’d whisper to me who killed Trisha Maples.

But then Leo and Chanelle look mighty guilty.

The shoe that was left in the parking lot the night of the murder—the one that was mysteriously retrieved, comes back to me.

I’m betting Chanelle Maples happens to own a pair just like them.

I’ve seen it before—a couple teams up to off the competition.

But this time the competition just happens to be the mother of the soon-to-be bride.

How could Chanelle do something so monstrous?

How could she?

16

The days grow shorter, and the nights grow impossibly long and desperately cold. It always seems that November melts away far faster than necessary. At the juncture we're at now, it feels like a race to Thanksgiving—and it is. The big cornucopia-filled day is just two sleeps away.

It's the afternoon of Trisha Maples' funeral, and the skies are filled with dark-bellied clouds ready to lance themselves open and pour out a deluge upon our world. Honey Hollow Covenant Church was brimming with bodies, the tears were plentiful, and soon enough the entire congregation moves over to the hall conjoined to the church where there will be refreshments and people can try to process their bereavement.

Carlson Hall has played host to wedding receptions, baptismal celebrations, and even hosted a birthday party or two, but it seems as of late all we've hosted here have been funerals.

Lily comes my way with an armful of platters, mostly chocolate chip cookies, sugar cookies in the shapes of pumpkins and turkeys to add a tiny festive touch, pumpkin bars, and brownies, too.

"I think that's it, Lottie." Lily blows a stray lock of hair out of her eyes. "That was very nice of you to offer to provide the cookie trays for free."

"It's the least I could do," I say. "After all, I found the poor woman." Besides, I would never say this out loud, but you never know what kind of information you could glean at a funeral. I figure most of the suspects should be here. And if anything else, I can get another chance to have a conversation with them. But Detective Ivy Fairbanks will inevitably be here, too. She and Noah used to do the funereal sweeps themselves, keeping both an ear and eye out on the suspects at large.

Noah.

My heart breaks just thinking about him. He still thinks I'm having Everett's baby. That must be killing him—no pun intended.

I turn toward the door as the crowd keeps funneling in and I see a tall and brightly illuminated specter with glowing green eyes and dimples staring right at me.

"*Noah!*" I practically leap in the air at the sight of him. And just like that, he blinks out of existence.

"*Geez,* Lottie!" Lily clutches at her chest. "You nearly gave me a heart attack. One corpse is enough for the venue, thank you very much."

A couple of women turn our way, shocked by Lily's crass words.

"I'm sorry," I hiss. "I was just thinking about him." My hand rides to my belly.

If Noah comes back, I'm going to tell him about the baby. I don't want to whisper the news into the ear of his seemingly lifeless body. I want to see his face light up myself. But then I suppose it's already lit up supernaturally without my assistance, but nevertheless I want to look into his eyes when I tell him we're about to expand our family. Noah and I are already a family. We just passed our two-month anniversary without a whimper.

Lily hitches a dark strand of hair behind her ear, her features softening my way. "I'm sorry you're going through this, Lottie. Maybe you should spend more time with Everett to get your mind off things for a while? Grieving Noah like this can be extremely stressful." She spots someone in the crowd and points their way. "Look at Cormack."

I crane my neck until I find her pawing all over Topper Blakley.

Lily leans in. "She's found someone to lean on. Trust me, and take a page out of Cormack's book. That's what you need. Or you'll just lose your mind and start shouting Noah's name for no reason at all."

"Funny. But I'm not taking anything out of Cormack's book. It's probably written backwards and she's reading it upside down."

"Think about it," she says, taking the keys to the van from me. "I'm heading back to the bakery. I'll see you later. Hitch a ride home with Everett." She nods behind me. "Before he moves onto someone else."

I turn and find Everett with his own blonde pawing all over him. I'm about to head over when I nearly knock the coffee right out of some poor girl's hand.

"Oh, I'm so sorry!" I help stabilize the Styrofoam cup before looking up, only to find Annette Havershem. "Annette—I mean, Nettie." It bubbles from me unexpectedly. After all, she did invite me to use her nickname that last time we met. "I'm surprised to see you here. That was very nice of you to come."

She averts her eyes. "I'm here because my aunt asked me to. And I like Chanelle." She shrugs. Her hair is swept up into a partial ponytail, partial chignon combo and she has a trio of rhinestones pushed in just above her ear. She has on a dark stole and a dark dress, and even if she's not grieving Trisha, she sure is playing the part.

"That's really kind of you. I had a chance to meet Chanelle. She seems really nice. It's a shame she and her mother didn't get along."

Her chest bounces as she swallows down a laugh. "How could they? Chanelle had so much pent-up vengeance against her mother she actually snatched that cheesy boyfriend out from under her."

Ha. She just collaborated Jade's story. So it's true. Chanelle was hiding something from me. I wonder what else she's hiding?

A thought comes to me. Chanelle says she saw Trisha and Leo arguing. I myself saw Leo dragging Trisha away. I wonder if that's enough evidence for Ivy to interrogate Leo further?

I spot him across the room as he laughs it up with my mother. My goodness, my mother had better not even think of tacking him onto her already colorful lineup of suitors.

"Nettie?" I lean in before doing a quick sweep of the vicinity. "Did you happen to see Leo arguing with Trisha just before she was murdered? Or maybe with your aunt? Something really upset her and sent her running for the parking lot."

"No." She shudders as if reliving a bad memory. "Actually, my aunt mentioned something about getting a sweater out of Trisha's car. I guess she left it at the shelter and Trisha picked it up for her. They often break a sweat while working in the kitchen and my aunt is notorious for wearing five or six layers. I'm just glad she didn't go out there with a killer on the loose. I don't know what I'd do if I lost Aunt Gerrie."

Gerrie needed something from the parking lot? A lure maybe?

I scan the hall for her, but the crowd is so thick it's like looking for a gray-headed needle in a silver haystack.

"Nettie, you don't think Chanelle had anything to do with this, do you?"

She inches back as if I had just threatened her. "Are you kidding? Trisha and Chanelle might not have gotten along, but she's not a killer." She glares at someone across the room. "And contrary to popular opinion, neither am I."

I follow her gaze all the way to Jade Pope and Chanelle.

"I'll see you at the shelter in a couple of days, Lottie. You'll have to excuse me. I have someone to speak to." She takes off in a huff, and I turn around and head straight for Everett to find the blonde bimbo still trying to adhere herself to his side.

"Everett," I say brightly as I take up his hand.

His eyes enlarge for a moment. "Cressie was just talking about how she's fallen on hard times."

"*Cressie*?" I ask, amused—and, okay, I'm a little bit perturbed by the fact he's throwing out old nicknames.

His lips cinch to the side as if to apologize, and I shoot her the side-eye. Her floor-length royal blue dress says formal, but that flirty slit that runs all the way up to her thighs—on both sides—screams sleazy nightclub in Leeds.

"That's right." Cressida's head lolls my way. Her hair shines like platinum, her pretty blue eyes have a glassy appeal, and her skin looks so luminescent that if I didn't know better, I'd bet she were dead. But I'm not that lucky.

I frown at my own poor taste. Of course, I don't wish the girl was dead, but is a faint memory too much to ask for?

Cormack pops up, sans her new sugar daddy. Her microscopic little black dress looks more appropriate for clubbing than a funeral, but then I suppose she didn't quite know Trisha as well as she knew Chanelle perhaps. Honestly, I have no idea why she's here.

I glance back and find that Topper already has another blonde strapped to his side—my mother.

Great. Who would have thought that Cormack could end up in a love triangle with both my mother *and* me? I suppose I should warn my sisters—Meg at least.

Cormack gives an enthusiastic hop. "What did I miss?"

I press a wry smile at Everett. "*Cressie* was just about to fill us in on her misfortune." I shoot a look to the scheming socialite who's trying her best to snag my man. "Spill it."

Cressida grunts to her old friend, "I've had a terrible run of bad luck as you know." She turns to Everett. "I've had to cut back to three vacations a year."

Cormack sucks in a quick breath. "Oh, Cressie. I know you had it tough, but I had no idea it was that bad. Why didn't you say anything? Daddy would have gladly stepped in to save the day. No one would ever want to see you living this way."

Cormack's level of generosity brings new meaning to *brother, can you spare a diamond?*

"Wow," I muse. "Just three? How ever will you survive? May I ask where you're heading this year?"

She whimpers as if it were truly painful to discuss. "Somewhere tropical in April and May. Europe for the summer and Vail from January through March."

My mouth falls open. She calls that a vacation? I'd call that moving three times a year.

Everett's chest rumbles with a dull laugh. "I haven't had a vacation in eons."

Cressida pulls his tie forward in one lusty move. "Oh, please come with. I have so much room at the chalet. It's a shame to let all that space go to waste. So far, it's just me and thirty-two of my closest friends."

I lean in, waiting for some clue that this is all just a put-on, but she's as serious as that gunshot wound that landed us all here today.

Everett winces. "I'm afraid I'll have to pass. It's pretty challenging getting a few months off from the courthouse."

Cressida clicks her tongue. "I never did understand why you took such a blue-collar job to begin with."

Since when was a judge considered blue collar? And what's wrong with blue-collar jobs anyway?

Cressida gasps as if she just had a brainstorm. "There's still room for you on the sailing circuit, you know. I hear Kippy has a space available on his team. You used to love to race."

"I didn't know that about you." I wrap my arms around Everett and he pulls me in close. "And did you really hang out with a guy named Kippy?"

His lids hood low. "Do I lose points if I say yes?"

"Maybe," I tease.

He looks to Cressida. "The racing sounds wonderful, but I'm afraid my line of work doesn't allow for that either. But what it does allow for"— his chest expands between us— "is a nice three-day weekend stay at the Maple Meadows Lodge in just a couple of weeks."

Cormack coos at the two of us. "How perfectly romantic. Is that a cozy cottage in France somewhere?"

Everett looks dismayed by the thought. "It's in Hollyhock."

And just like that, a giant explosion of light ricochets around the room, and standing before us is Noah— questionably alive and well, and sans the flesh.

I give Everett's hand a hard squeeze as if to alert him to the fact. I'm not sorry to say we'll have to cut short our time with the silver spoon sisters.

Cormack screams as if she just saw Noah herself, and I'm more than mildly alarmed.

"I just remembered something." She leans our way. "I saw the two of you leaving the Diamond Stop just as I was headed in. Minerva let me know that the two of you were trying on engagement rings!"

I gasp as my eyes meet up with Noah's and I shake my head, trying to refute the idea.

Cormack bubbles with laughter. "And then, of course, I spotted you coming out of Redwood Realty. A ring *and* a house? Everett, did you knock this girl up or something?"

Noah sighs. His shoulders sag in defeat as he quickly begins to dissipate.

"Noah, wait!" I call out and all eyes are suddenly on me.

Both Cormack and Cressida turn in the direction I'm howling in as if they were expecting to see him, too.

"Oh shoot," Cormack grunts while looking back at what looks to be an argument brewing between Chanelle, Jade, and Nettie. "For a second there, I thought you said 'Noah, wait,' but now I see you said '*no, wait*.' If you'll excuse me, I need to break this up."

Cressida groans, "I'll help, but I'd better not break a nail."

They take off and another celestial entity strides up in their wake. It's Gemma making her way over with her usual animalistic swagger, her neck jutting to and fro every other step.

"Oh heavens. I've missed it, haven't I?" She bats those long lashes as she gives a quick look around the vicinity.

"You didn't miss much," I say, looking up at Everett. "But Noah was here for less than a moment. He heard that stuff about the engagement ring and the house, and I guess he couldn't take it anymore. I'm going to have to go to the hospital and tell him my secret, Everett."

He takes a quick breath. "I was hoping he could hear the news in person. I mean without his person—in his ghostly form."

Gemma takes a few steps forward. "Why, it looks as if a brawl is breaking out. And at a funeral of all places. Some people have no respect for the dead."

We glance over to see Chanelle trying to hold Annette back. And Cormack is restraining Jade.

"Something is definitely afoot."

Before Everett can respond, a tall redheaded detective with a swath of crimson lipstick bears her fangs our way.

"What's next in your investigation, *Lemon*?" Ivy doesn't mind one bit smearing with sarcasm the nickname Everett has lovingly gifted me.

"Investigation? What investigation?" I bat my lashes at her innocently. "Last I checked, you're the trained professional." I no sooner get the words out than Gemma brays out a storm of laughter.

"Are you close to making an arrest?" I ask.

Ivy sniffs the air while looking into the crowd.

"Why yes, I am, Lottie. You worry about the pies. I'll worry about catching the bad guys. Let's just say this. By Thanksgiving, Trisha Maples' family will have a lot to be thankful for indeed."

Everett and I exchange a glance.

Gemma makes a strangled yelping sound as she bucks and kicks her way through the crowd with glee.

Ivy seems confident she's got the killer, and I'm morbidly curious as to who this might be.

My gaze drifts to the squabbling trio in the back getting ready to throw punches. Next to them stands none other than Leo Workman, his arms folded with confidence as he speaks with my mother and Topper.

Both Ivy and Leo seem unduly confident in something, and I'm beginning to wonder if they're on a collision course with each other.

I suppose it would be convenient to wrap up the investigation before Thanksgiving.

But something tells me justice isn't always convenient.

17

Thanksgiving arrives with all the pomp and circumstance this turkey-riddled day deserves.

In what turned out to be a beautiful avalanche of generosity, once my mother and sisters heard about me helping out at the shelter this afternoon, they too volunteered to help out—and so did Carlotta, Hook, Forest, Keelie, Bear, Alex, Lily, and Naomi. It's a full house of Honey Hollow townies helping out those in need of a hand down in Leeds.

The shelter kitchen and dining room are expansive in size and remind me a lot of the gym back at Honey Hollow High. There are scores of elongated tables set out with pumpkins, fall flowers, and cornucopias lining the centers of them. Young kids are running around and laughing, and everyone in line waiting to be served is engaged in lively conversation. It's a darn right festive atmosphere, as it should be.

I'm dressed head to foot in my fall finery, an emerald green cardigan with matching turtleneck, a pair of cranberry jeans with extra stretch for added comfort, and, of course, I have Ethel, my handy Glock, in a small leather backpack strapped to me. Everett suggested I bring her, and I couldn't say no. Okay, so he may have insisted, but I didn't resist. He's right. There will be a lot of people here today, and Ivy has all but made me a target. It's better to be safe than sorry.

Once I finish slicing up a million pumpkin pies, I make my way out to the food line, only to see a sexy judge doling out mashed potatoes with the best of them.

I head on over and wrap my arms around him from the back.

"Do you know how hot it is to see a man who's not afraid to roll up his sleeves?"

He lifts a brow as he turns my way. "About as hot as it is to see a baker running a knife wildly through her pies? I had a straight shot of you from here and it was quite a sight. You didn't lose a finger, did you?"

"Nope. But I did burn some serious calories. I can't wait to dive into all this delicious food and put them right back where they belong."

"Good. And I'm glad to see you have that special purse attached to your body."

The special purse is the tiny backpack my sister bought me last Christmas. It's a bit of a showstopper itself with its black leather and silver buckles. Little did Lainey know it would one day become a glorified gun holster.

Mom comes up from behind. "Don't you dare eat one ounce of this feast. This is for those less fortunate than us, Lottie. Our feast is being delivered by the Honey Pot Diner at six, straight to the B&B. Don't be late, you two!" She takes off with an armful of rolls as she makes her way to the end of the line.

A spasm of light goes off in the kitchen, and every last cell in my body is hopeful that it's Noah.

Everett and I spent nearly all day yesterday with him at the hospital. Everett rehashed every story from their short tenure as stepbrothers out loud, and I laughed as he entertained me with one tale after the next. I could have sworn I saw Noah's eyebrows bounce a few times in amusement himself, but the nurse says that was more than likely an automatic bodily response.

The light begins to quicken as the hall behind the kitchen grows brighter.

"Excuse me. I'd better check on my pies." I feel a wee bit bad about not telling Everett the supernatural truth, but I'll make sure to check the pies just so that I'm not officially lying to him.

I make my way to the back of the kitchen and spot Gemma doing an odd little dance. That tuft of fluffy hair at the top of her hair bounces with her every move and her mouth hangs open, exposing me to more of her buck-toothed cuteness.

"Something is happening, Lottie. What is it? What is it?" Her voice grows more spastic by the moment.

"I don't know," I say as I crane my neck back at the service line. Down at the opposite end of where Everett and my mother are, I spot Chanelle standing right next to Leo and my stomach drops.

How dare she tell me she has no idea who he is and then so brazenly step out with him in public the very same week her mother was buried.

I didn't even know Trisha that way, and I'm fuming as I make my way over.

"Chanelle," I say as cheerful as I can muster. "What a surprise to see you here."

Her lips twist with a precocious smile. "My mother used to ask me at least once a month to make the effort, but as long as she was here, I knew I didn't want to be." She takes a brief break from doling out the green beans. "But a friend asked me to come." She shoots a sly glance to Leo who's become quite animated and friendly toward the people he's serving ever since I showed up.

"A friend?" I skewer him with a look. "I thought you said you didn't know your mother's boyfriend?"

She shrugs it off as if it were no big deal. "The weird thing is, she knew I had my sights set on him." Her lids lower just a notch. "That's just another typical example of what a great mother she was. Anyway, that's over for good now." She shudders. "And you know what? I'm ready to start life all over again. In fact, I might even start volunteering here at the shelter more often."

Gerrie Havershem walks by at a quickened clip carrying an empty oversized pot back to the kitchen. Now there's a suspect I haven't pinned down yet.

"Have a good time," I say to Chanelle just as someone demands their green beans.

I trot ahead of Gerrie and take the empty, albeit still heavy, oversized stockpot.

"I've got it," I say as I step in stride with her. "Things are really going well today."

"That they are, and they wouldn't be without your pies. I can't believe Nettie got you to donate with just a quick word. Usually we have to beg and pester people about donations. And yet, here you are, not only with pies, but with friends and family to help serve the masses. I can't tell you what a blessing you've been."

Her silver hair is neatly curled under her jawline and she's wearing a burnt umber wool sweater with matching shell. There's just something about her that reminds me of my mother, and a part of me can never envision her pulling the trigger to end anyone's life—even if she was having a beef with them.

I set the pot down on the counter in the kitchen.

"I bet you miss Trisha," I say, although I'm not quite sure she does. "I mean, at the shelter. She was a big helper I hear."

"Oh." She averts her eyes. "She was something. Okay, so she was a helper. But she was a control freak, too. I don't know how many times she tried to berate me on the way I operated things around here."

There was a time or two I witnessed her doing the same thing to Naomi, so this doesn't surprise me.

"I'm sure it came as a great shock to hear she was murdered."

She sniffs the air. "I wish I could say I was surprised. That woman made an enemy or six before noon each day. Not all of us know how to play well with others on this planet."

Cormack and Cressida bounce through my mind.

"I'll second that." A thought comes to me. "Hey? It's so hot in here I'd love to take off my sweater, but I'm afraid I'll leave it here." My finger glides over the strap from my backpack as I feel Ethel warming me from behind. "It was my father's favorite on me and I'd hate to lose it." And I hate that I just dragged my deceased father into my investigation unwittingly. But, knowing my father, he'd be glad to help.

Gerrie's robust upper torso bounces with a laugh, her chin rippling with the effect. "I've done it a time or two." Her expression grows dark. "In fact, it almost cost me my life."

"What?" I gasp just enough to let her know I'm more than interested.

"That's right. The night Trisha was killed." She leans in. "I left my sweater right here at the shelter and Trisha brought it over to me. It was still in her car while I was fixing to leave. And Nettie, being the sweet angel she is, asked Trisha for her keys so I wouldn't have to face her after the disagreement we had."

"What kind of disagreement?"

She clamps her lips shut before turning to her left. "Even though we often didn't get along, I wanted to let her know that there was another woman her beau was seeing. I mean, if it were me, I'd want to know. Wouldn't you?"

"You bet I would."

"I didn't tell her who. I just simply hinted at it, but after she made that snide remark about me not being able to handle being in charge of the volunteers, my niece leaned in and whispered it to her. You could have blown Trisha down with a philandering feather."

"So do you know who the other woman was?" I bite down on my lip because I feel bad for asking. It feels more like gossiping.

"Oh yes." She rolls her eyes to the ceiling. "That saucy daughter of hers. She's known for stirring the pot."

"That would explain why Nettie and Jade were going at it in her midst," I muter under my breath.

"At the funeral?" Gerrie shakes her head. "Oh, those girls have a genuine tiff of their own. Jade does anyhow. I personally think my niece is the innocent in all this."

"How so?"

She glances over my shoulder before leaning in. "Nettie used to date Jade's brother Robby."

"The one who passed away?"

She gives a sorrowful nod. "Of course, Jade blames Nettie for everything that happened to the man, but none of it was her fault, I tell you."

"What happened to him?"

"Robby Pope—well, he was a scoundrel. A charming scoundrel nevertheless. Once their parents died, Robby turned to a life of crime to help support both him and his sister. Nettie was dating him in the midst of all this. Anyway, they arrested him for grand larceny and put him away for what would have been quite some time, but he was killed in prison."

"That's terrible all around. How especially sad that he felt a life of crime was his only alternative."

"Theft is never the answer." She takes a breath as she looks out at the crowd in the dining room. "But then neither is murder."

She takes off, and I'm about to head that way myself when I hear a loud pop come from just outside the door that leads to the alley. That's exactly where I parked my van.

Good grief. It had better not have gotten hit. I love every inch of that van and coincidentally the man who gifted it to me. I'm sure Everett wouldn't be too happy to see it smashed up either.

I head on out into the frigid air and spot a body lying next to the dumpsters.

"Oh my goodness," I shout as I head over to find Nettie Havershem lying on her back, her eyes wide open, a crimson bloom expanding over the center of her chest as she shivers uncontrollably.

"Nettie?" I call out as I run to her side and a small group of women pour out of the kitchen along with me.

"Call 911," I shout and one of them whips out her phone as the others quickly tend to Nettie.

Oh my goodness, I have to call Noah. I mean, Everett. I should call Ivy, too, but my phone isn't on me at the moment.

The sound of heels clattering away comes from behind the building. And without thinking I bolt on over.

The shadow of a woman gets lost among the forest just to my left, and I traverse the debris in the woods in an effort to catch up with her. My word, she could be the killer.

My heart begins to race, and my adrenaline takes off to new heights.

The woman trips over a log and I close in on her, spinning her around by the arm, and before I can see her face my eyes hook over her shoes a moment.

I gasp at the navy heels with a thick gold band over the toe. I look up slowly and meet her gaze.

"It was you that night. You killed Trisha Maples. And you just shot Nettie, too."

18

There is always an odd sense of satisfaction when I finally peg down who the killer really is. There is a sense of excitement, the undeniable rush of adrenaline like I'm having now, and the undeniable sense of danger, which is always unavoidable.

I can feel Ethel lying over my back as that tiny backpack she's buried in warms my flesh. I was more than ambivalent about bringing my gun to the shelter today. I knew there would be kids, and lots and lots of families—but boy, am I ever glad I listened to Everett and brought her anyway.

Although, at the moment, Jade Pope happens to have her own gun still clutched in her hand. And everyone knows one in the hand is better than one over the back.

"You did it," I say weakly. "But I know a great defense attorney who can spin this. I promise, Jade. You can plead insanity. You didn't mean to kill Trisha that night, did you?"

Her face grows increasingly pale as the woods lengthen their afternoon shadows over us. Jade's cat eyes only seem to grow more animalistic as the seconds go by. She's so beautiful, and smart—she didn't need to resort to this. But sadly, she did.

"How do you know?" She takes a step back, steadily raising the barrel my way. "Move slowly to your left. I'm a good shot, Lottie, as you can see." She looks sick at the thought as she glances quickly in the direction where Nettie lies—hopefully, getting the help she needs. "Start walking and start talking. Put your hands where I can see them. I'm curious to see if you got it right."

I lift my hands and do as I'm told, walking incredibly slowly toward the woods, backwards, just praying Everett will come looking for me.

"Talk, Lottie," she riots. The gun in her hand begins to waver as she becomes increasingly shaken.

An ambulance roars in this direction and her eyes widen with fear.

"Fine," I say a notch too loud myself. "You must have overheard the fact that Nettie was going to get Gerrie's jacket out of the car. You thought you had her alone, didn't you?"

"Yes." Her chest trembles with a silent laugh. "But what you don't realize is that as Trisha's assistant, I was at the shelter with her that afternoon. And once that old bat took her sweater off like she did every single time she was here"—she takes a moment to scoff—"I hid it so when it came time to leave, it was out of sight out of mind. It was my idea to take it to her. Trisha was a bit more vindictive and wanted to donate it to one of the women looking for a handout. And once it was safely in the back of Trisha's car, I knew she'd leave it there. It was me who told Nettie that she should get it. But what I didn't count on was the fact Trisha would intercept her and try to get it herself. Leo was breaking up with her and she wanted to leave. I overhead him telling her how smothered she made him feel. Anyone would have wanted to get out of that conversation."

That night comes back in snatches. "Both Trisha and Nettie had their hair up that evening."

She nods. "Now you're catching on. And they both wore red dresses. The lighting was terrible and my adrenaline had hit its zenith. I was finally going to take that witch off the planet for what she did to my family."

"To your brother?" I nod, casually letting my backpack swing off my left shoulder.

I'm so close to Ethel, I can feel her.

"Yes"—she cries out in agony—"to my sweet Robby." She tips her head back for a moment and lets out a howl of grief.

I land my backpack in my hand, my fingers on the zipper.

"Oh, Lottie, you don't know what it feels like to lose someone you love. It guts you—it changes you right down to the core of who you are. I had to go through it three times,

Lottie. First with my parents. But Robby—he shouldn't have died. He wouldn't have gone to prison if Nettie hadn't been such a princess. My word, he felt the constant need to spoil her. All she wanted was expensive purses and shoes."

I glance down at her heels. "You lost a shoe that night, didn't you?" I say breathless as a white plume expels from my mouth. It's so cold and dank, I'm shivering right to the bone.

She stills a moment as if in awe of me. "You really do notice everything, don't you? Yes, I lost a shoe, but only for a minute. My heel caught in the concrete, but I kept running. I heard voices out in the parking lot, and I didn't want anyone to see me. And as soon as the deputies arrived, and the melee picked up, I went back and retrieved it. I thought I was going to get caught that same night. And yet, it was today— and it wasn't by the sheriff's department at all. It was you. Some silly little baker sticking her nose where it doesn't belong." She gives a long blink, her chest palpitating hard. "And now I'm going to have to kill again, Lottie. I'm sorry, but I have to do this. Whatever it is you need to say, you have three seconds. Speak your final words."

The forest lights up with a burst of supernatural light and Gemma comes charging out from the right and straight for Jade.

Oh, thank goodness. Once Gemma knocks her over, I'll pull Ethel out and shoot if I have to. I've killed before—and I'm not afraid to do it again.

But for whatever reason, Gemma doesn't knock Jade down. In fact, Jade doesn't even budge. Instead, Gemma goes right through Jade like the ghost she is.

"Oh dear!" Gemma canters back. "I'm afraid I don't know how to move anything, Lottie. I'm a failure of a ghost, and soon you'll be as dead as I am."

I'd tell her to go find Carlotta, the only other supersensual I know, but I'm half-afraid Gemma might get distracted in the process. No offense, but her track record doesn't bode well.

I spot a long evergreen branch under Jade's left foot and hitch my head toward it to Gemma.

"I'm on it, Lottie! She'll be airborne before you know it!"

Gemma tugs and bites and pushes, but the branch isn't fazed by her ghostly shenanigans.

Jade squints over at me. "What do you keep looking at? I'm sorry, Lottie, but you've wasted your time. Get ready to meet your maker. And if you can, please tell Trisha I'm sorry. And tell Robby that I love him."

The powerfully loud pop of the gun goes off like an explosion just as the woods light up as bright as noonday, and the next thing I know Jade Pope is on the ground, her gun more than five feet from her as she does her best to crawl over to it.

"Lottie!" a familiar deep voice calls out, and I look up to find the most dashing poltergeist of them all—the father of my child, my sweet prince, Noah. "Kick the gun away and run!"

I try to do just that, but Jade grabs me by the ankle and yanks me down, causing me to fall right over her.

"*Lottie,*" Noah roars. "Be careful—the baby!"

Jade wrestles me to the ground and wraps her hands around my neck. I do my best to pry her fingers off, but she's got a vise grip over me. Her eyes are wild with despair.

Noah lets out a growl and lifts Jade right off my body. He hoists her into the air before she slips right through his ghostly fingers.

Gemma speeds over and miraculously breaks Jade's fall by inadvertently offering her a piggyback ride.

Jade's face grows white with shock once she realizes she's floating through the air and she passes right out.

"Noah!" I jump to my feet and wrap my arms around him before he has the chance to disappear. "Oh, Noah, I need you. I love you so much. Please don't leave me." I land a smoldering kiss to his lips and I feel him there, kissing me right back.

He pulls away slowly.

"I miss you, too, Lottie. Every minute of every day. I'm sorry about leaving that night you met my mother, and I'm sorry about my mother. But I don't have much control over anything. It seems when I get upset, I get evicted from the scene."

Jade moans as she slowly comes to, but I choose to ignore her for now.

"That's because it's not good for you to be upset." I close my eyes a moment. "Noah, I have news," I say, shaking my head at him, tears in my eyes. "This baby I'm carrying—it's not Everett's. It's yours."

"What?" he says it breathless as he pulls back. His glowing green eyes look down toward my belly. "Mine?"

"Yes," I pant it out with a laugh. "It's ours. Everett and I aren't engaged, and we didn't buy a house. We're buying the lodge up in Hollyhock—for you. Once you wake up, we can straighten the whole thing out."

"Lottie, I don't know what to say." His eyes light up ten times brighter than before as he takes me in from head to toe. "You're so beautiful inside and out, I want nothing more than to have a family with you."

"It's happening. The baby is already on its way."

"It's happening." His dimples dig in, and then he begins to fade. "I'm sorry, Lottie. I think the news overwhelmed me. The last thing I ever want to do is leave you." His voice is the last to fade, and just like that, he's gone.

"Lottie!" Gemma begins to buck wildly. "Something is happening! Oh dear. I'm afraid I've gone too far." Gemma's ghostly frame begins to fade just as quickly as Noah did. "Take good care of that baby, Lottie Lemon! And good work catching the killer!"

The woods clap to darkness and Jade falls to the ground with an unceremonious thump.

"Lottie?" Everett's voice booms from the alley, and soon enough I'm wrapped safely in his arms as the woods fill with deputies.

They take Jade Pope in for the murder of Trisha Maples and the attempted murder of Annette Havershem.

"I couldn't save either of them from being shot," I whisper to Everett as I look up at his brilliant blue eyes. "I wish I could have saved two people."

"You did save two people." He presses his penetrative gaze to mine. "You saved yourself and your baby." His cheek flickers up one side. "Would it worry you too much if I never left your side for the next eight months? You've already shaved ten years off the back end of my life. I couldn't stand if anything happened to either of you."

A sad laugh trembles from me, and I shake my head as tears come to my eyes. "I love the way you love me."

"Good. Because I love you both."

My lips invert as I stave off the urge to blubber right here in a forest crawling with sheriff's deputies.

"I saw Noah and I told him. He knows." The words come from me, threadbare. "He knows I'm having his baby."

His lips curl in the right direction, and it might be the very first official smile I have ever seen on this man—or at least one that has lasted this long.

"Good. I'm glad. Now maybe he'll fight like hell to get back to both of you."

"He better."

Everett lands a kiss to my forehead. "I'm guessing Ivy will want to speak with you. I'll make sure it's quick. You need your rest."

"And my Thanksgiving dinner."

Everett and I head out with his strong arm around me, protecting me, shielding me, making me feel both very safe and loved.

With Noah and Everett in my life, I have a lot to be thankful for indeed.

Now to find a way to keep Noah in my life, in the flesh, and in this baby's life, too.

Something has to go our way for once.

And this had better be it.

19

It all happens in a blur, Ivy requesting I come down to the station, Everett zipping us back to the bakery afterwards to pick up pies to take to my mother's, heading home to change my clothes and feed my sweet cats their special Thanksgiving feast I picked up at the pet store for just the occasion, and then finally landing at the B&B.

Ivy texted a few minutes ago and let me know Nettie is in stable condition and that she wouldn't be pressing charges against me for interfering in her investigation—this time. Considering the fact she was ready to arrest Leo Workman, you'd think she'd pen me a thank you for saving her the trouble.

I wipe all of that out of my head for now. I've got an armful of pies and a gorgeous man by my side. All I want to do tonight is focus on the ones I love while I fill my stomach with all the deliciousness this day has to offer.

No sooner do Everett and I make our way through the entry of the B&B than I spot Greer and Winslow, the two friendly ghosts that love to tear and scare up the halls. They're standing there along with Carlotta, having a chortling good time.

Everett's arms are loaded with pies, and I tell him to go ahead and set them in the kitchen.

"You got it," he says as he looks to the woman who bore me. "Don't you let her out of your sight, Carlotta."

"That's Sawyer to you!" she calls after him and we share a little laugh. "So do you feel the kiddo squirming yet? I bet you're green around the gills each morning like I was. Although it just so happens, I was green around the gills all day long no thanks to your inability to tell time."

"I apologize. And no, oddly I feel fine. I mean, I feel tired. But I've baked about a thousand pies in the last week alone. That kind of workout could bring even a seasoned athlete to their knees."

"I don't doubt it."

Greer lets out a ghostly howl as her dark hair glitters like onyx. "So it's true?"

Winslow laughs and his voice sounds perfectly hollow. He's so handsome and dapper looking today with his light brown hair slicked back, and his dark suit looks newer but still more appropriate for a Thanksgiving taking place about two hundred years ago.

"Of course, it's true," he hums. "She's glowing. A woman always glows when she's with child."

Greer shakes her head. "She's glowing because she's madly in love with that sexy man who came bearing pies."

"I am, but he's not the father."

Both Greer and Winslow gasp just as little Lea and my favorite black cat, Thirteen, bound over.

"Has it happened?" Lea calls out. "Have you had that baby yet?" she snips the words as if the thought were an irritant to her.

Thirteen lets out a yodeling howl, his fur sparkling with black and silver stars, and he looks like magic personified.

"No, she hasn't had it yet." He wraps himself around my ankles, and I can feel his fur as sure as if he were here in the flesh. "It takes an eon or two before a human can produce a healthy litter. The little kittens haven't formed a single whisker as of yet at this stage." His tail lights up a sparkling shade of deep purple. "Have they, Lottie?"

"You're right, but they won't be forming whiskers, and I'm pretty sure there is just one little human brewing in here. I've yet to go to the doctor, but I'm determined to make an appointment bright and early in the morning."

Greer whimpers, "I'm so happy for you, Lottie. And I just know that Everett will make a great father."

"Noah," I correct. "I did say that, right?"

"You did," she affirms while pulling Winslow in close. "But we already know that Everett will be an important part of your life, Lottie."

"He will," I assert without a doubt, and yet there's a twinge of sadness in my heart. "I just hate how complicated everything has become."

Carlotta honks out a laugh. "I wouldn't sweat it," she says, waving the ghosts around us to the dining room as she navigates us all that way. "You've got a man for each arm, Lottie. Nothing wrong with that. A man for each side of the bed, too. Some people call that living your best life."

I can't help but scoff. "And some people call that a fantasy that should never test the boundaries of reality—i.e., my mother."

"Who are you kidding, Lottie? Your mother would be the first to approve of that raunchy arrangement. Have you read her book? She happened to give me an advanced copy. I'd be worried of what the townsfolk might think if I were you."

"Since when have you worried about what others think?"

"I said if I were you."

We head into the main dining hall of the B&B, and it's decorated from top to bottom in festive fall leaves, wreaths, pine cones, and pumpkins hollowed out with a bouquet of sunflowers blooming out of them.

"Oh, Mom, you've gone overboard!" I pull her into a quick embrace. The room is brimming with people, family, friends, and B&B boarders alike. Meg, Lainey, and their plus ones, my new half-sisters Kelleth and Aspen, Mayor Nash and his ex-Chrissy, Keelie, Bear, Naomi, Lily, Finn and Britney, Alex and his mother Suze, Cormack and her friends Larson and Cressida. I can't help but scowl at that last one.

"Thank you, Lottie." Mom leans in. "But it's all smoke and mirrors. After I found out what you went through, I couldn't stop shaking. Chrissy and Keelie did all of this on their own."

Keelie bops over and wraps her arms around me, and I feel the prickling of tears underneath my eyelids because I've yet to break my news to my very best friend—to anyone really. Not on purpose anyway.

"Lottie Lemon." Keelie pulls back and holds out a sparkler on her left ring finger. "Thank you. Bear told me that you went in and helped him out a bit."

Bear pops up from behind her and winces. "She dragged it out of me."

"Hey, Everett and I just narrowed down the field," I say. "The rest was all him."

I pull her hand forward and admire the cushion cut diamond that catches the light in the room and holds it hostage, as it should.

"It's amazing." Tears sting my eyes once again, and this time they're all for Keelie. "Just like the two of you."

Becca, Chrissy Nash, and my mother swoop over, and soon they're all swooning and admiring Bear's wonderful taste in diamonds.

I turn and spin right into Kelleth and Aspen, along with Cormack and her snobby friends, Larson and Cressida. This is one gaggle of blondes I want nothing to do with at the moment.

"Happy Thanksgiving," I say brightly as I try my best to duck on out of the awkward social situation.

"Whoa, Lottery." Cormack pulls me back. "We have a special request."

Larson looks down her nose at me quite literally. "Your sisters tell me that there's not a better baker in all of Vermont."

"Wow, thank you." I blink over at Kelleth and Aspen, suddenly feeling a bit guilty about wanting to ditch them so quickly. "I'm here for all your baking needs."

"Good." Larson zips a large pendant across the gold chain around her neck. "Because Cressie and I are throwing our annual Christmas party up on Garland Road. We'd like for you to bring your sweet treats. And Yule logs—lots of Yule logs for the guests to enjoy. That creme filled cake has become a tradition."

"Wow, Garland Road. That's a beautiful neighborhood." I happen to know that Garland Road is on the side of town where rows of ritzy mansions line the streets. "I would be honored to cater the party. I'll come bearing cookie platters and Yule logs alike. Just let me know the date and time."

Cressida snorts. "Of course."

Her eyes grow large as she lunges forward, and for a second, I think perhaps her pricy high heels are malfunctioning and she's about to topple on me, but she ends up slapping herself over the body that just popped up next to mine, Everett.

"Oh, Essex." She dots his face with manic kisses. "How could you possibly trade me in for someone who plays with flour and sugar all day long? Remember that time you told me that nothing tastes sweeter than my kisses?"

His eyes flit to mine, and there's a slightly guilty look on his face.

"That's adorable," I say, plucking her off of him and wrapping my own arms around him. "He says the same to me." I'm not sure if he's said quite those words, but we've had a few spicy verbal exchanges at precariously intimate moments and I do believe he mentioned the fact I taste like candy. Close enough.

Everett steals a moment to land his lips to my ear. "It's true. Have I mentioned how lately that I have a craving for candy?"

A fire rips through my insides, and I give Everett's hand a tiny pat as a reprimand for being so overtly naughty.

"Excuse us"—he says—"we need to speak with our realtor." He leads us over near the fireplace where my sisters congregate with Hook and Forest.

Forest has his arms wrapped around Lainey's body, his hand gently warming her belly sort of the way I'm doing to my own at the moment without thinking. Although it is Thanksgiving, I'm sure people will just assume I'm starved for all that good food, which I totally am.

Hook slaps Everett on the back. "Congratulations, you two. Escrow closes tomorrow. Come afternoon and you'll be the new owners of the Maple Meadows Lodge."

Lainey and Meg let out a couple of howls of approval.

Lainey balls up her fists with enthusiasm. "When do we go? I hear there's snow in the forecast, and I love me a good mountain getaway."

Everett cocks his head. "Whenever you wish. We've got more rooms than we know what to do with. And the entire place needs to be renovated."

Meg leans in. "I'm not picking up a paintbrush, but I'll help you style the rooms if you like. I've spent my fair share of nights in various Vegas hotel rooms. I know a thing or two about glitz and glamour."

"Sounds good. But let's keep it to a cozy cabin feel," I say.

Lainey wrinkles her nose. "Toss in a little glam for us girly girls, would you?"

Forest laughs. "And a moose head or two for us guys. You know, just to balance things out."

Lainey and Forest exchange a measured glance. And if I didn't know better, I'd say they were speaking to one another with their eyes.

"Come here." Lainey pulls Meg and me a touch closer. "I want to let you guys in on a little secret Forest and I have been keeping, but don't you dare tell Mom just yet. I have a cute surprise I'm going to give her in a bit." She swallows hard, tears suddenly sparkling in her eyes. "Forest and I are having a baby!" It comes out in an enthusiastic whisper, and both Meg and I wrap our arms around her, laughing and crying all at the very same time.

"A baby?" I mouth the words through tears. I glance to Everett and he gives a slight nod. "I wasn't going to bring it up, and I certainly don't want to take away from your moment, Lainey, so I'm not going to say a word to anyone but you guys—so you'll have to keep it a secret for now." I shoot a quick look to Hook and Forest, and they both offer a circular nod. "I'm having a baby, too," I whisper as my hands mold over my tummy.

"*What*?" Meg and Lainey hiss it out at once.

"You heard me. A baby." I press my lips tight. "It's Noah's." I glance over to the corner and spot his mother Suze laughing along with Alex.

My sisters' faces contort in horror.

Lainey is the first to pull me in. "Oh, honey. I don't know what to say."

"I do." Meg pulls me her way. "I always knew you'd get knocked up out of wedlock. I get twenty bucks from Mom and Lainey when you make it official."

"You were taking bets?" I swat her as she sheds a dark laugh.

Lainey shakes her head in disbelief, a smile frozen on her face. "When did you find out?"

"Funny story. I actually found out at your house, the day I went over to teach you to bake the pies. I went to the restroom and you had all these tests and I figured you wouldn't miss one. I'm sorry, but it was far too tempting. Anyway, I took it and set it behind the pumpkin on the counter—and when I came back later, it was positive. I just couldn't believe it."

Her mouth rounds out, but she's not saying a word.

"I'm so sorry, Lainey. I didn't mean to steal the test. I feel terrible just verbalizing it. I'll pay you back. I'm sure it was expensive. The darn thing all but talked to me."

"No"—she waves her arms as if that were the furthest thing from the truth—"it's not that. It's just that I hide the tests that I take behind the pumpkin, too. I mean, I was doing that all week." She cringes. "And, actually the day you came over is the day I took the test. That same night, in fact, while you were there. Lottie, are you sure you're pregnant? I mean, did you take another test?"

"No." I look to Everett in horror. "I thought one was enough."

"It is." Lainey shrugs. "Usually. The reason I'm asking is because I went into the bathroom after you did, and I happened to see a test back there. I just assumed it was mine from the day before." She winces. "Lottie, it was negative."

"What?" My heart plummets through the floor.

Lainey gives a weak nod. "Then I took another test, and right away it showed that I was pregnant. I hid it behind the pumpkin. I didn't tell you that night because I wanted Forest to be the first to know. And I've taken at least a half a dozen tests ever since. I'm due in August."

"Oh no." My hand floats over my mouth as I look to Everett. "I told Noah I was having his baby."

Everett closes his eyes a moment too long. "That's okay, Lemon. He'll understand."

Meg rubs my back. "If it's any consolation, he probably didn't hear you."

"Oh, he heard." And I got to see the wonderful look on his face. He was glowing—brighter than usual. "I'm so embarrassed. Could you all just do your best to forget every last bit of that?"

Everett pulls me in close, and I fight the urge to sob. Here I've fallen in love with a phantom child. We both had.

Dinner goes off without a hitch, but I can't help but be a little melancholy.

Afterwards, Keelie and Meg help me serve dessert, and everyone raves about how amazing the pies taste. I had three different varieties I baked last night just for the occasion—pumpkin, pecan, and sweet potato. Each one has my own little spin on it.

The party begins to break up and Noah's mother heads my way. I'll admit, there's a thin rail of fright riding through me. But then, she seems to have that effect on just about everyone.

Alex comes up to say goodnight, along with Lily and Naomi who actually have been carrying on conversations with one another without looking like they're going to kill one another.

Alex looks every bit like his older brother tonight. So much so it's scary. His dark hair is slicked back, his eyes are twinkling with delight, and every time those dimples of his go off, both Lily and Naomi moan and quiver. I can't say I blame them. It is quite a sight.

"So?" Everett looks to Alex. "What's the verdict? You said you'd choose by the end of the month between the two of these lovely ladies. Who's your new sidekick?"

"Oh." Lily raises a finger to Alex as if asking permission and he graciously extends a hand for her to continue. That's a new one. "We're switching off every other month like you, Lottie."

"Like me?" I inch back a notch. "Switching off every month? As in with Noah and Everett? I'm actually not doing that." Come to think of it, have I been doing that? "Not on purpose at least."

Naomi shrugs as if she were indifferent. "We're doing it, and that's all that matters. I get December."

Lily hikes a shoulder her way. "And he's starting off the new year the right way, with me."

"Wow, I don't know what to say." I shake my head in disbelief as I look to him. "Good luck, Alex. You're going to need it."

We share a warm laugh just as every ghost in this haunted B&B floats into the room and takes a seat on the enormous crystal chandelier.

The lights flicker as the monstrosity sways overhead and the room breaks out into spontaneous applause.

Mom hikes her glass up and others quickly do the same. "To the ghosts of the haunted Honey Hollow Bed and Breakfast!"

"Whoa, whoa!" Lainey tiptoes over in her heels and hands my mother a small navy felt box. "You might want to hold off on the toast for a second. Forest and I got you a little something."

"Ooh"—Mom's eyes grow swirly as she opens it carefully—"I love me a good present." She squints down at the contents of the box before her eyes grow to the size of baby rattles. "Oh my goodness! You're having a baby?"

Lainey nods her head with excitement as the room breaks out into cheers.

Forest helps my mother slip on the necklace that spells out *Grandma* in gold letters across the front. And as happy as I am for my sister, I can't help but mourn a little for the baby I thought I was having with Noah.

Suze comes up as if reading my mind.

"Everett"—she doesn't even bother looking my way—"I'll be seeing the doctor tomorrow. I know that my son wouldn't have wanted all these artificial life preserving measures. He was strong and robust and has no interest lying in a hospital bed for the rest of his life. We'll be discussing terminating his care." She nods curtly to Everett. "Please give your mother my best when you speak with her."

"*Everett.*" I can hardly press his name out. "I can't let her do that. I can't let her pull the plug." A thought comes to me. "You can't do that. I'm his wife. I'm legally the next of kin, and I'm not so much as pulling out a hair on his head." I'm filled with relief at the thought. Who knew our marriage would turn out to be a lifesaver? His.

"Hardly." She smacks her lips with disdain. "But I've consulted my legal team. I have the right to do as I wish."

Suze stalks out of the B&B and I'm frozen solid with anger.

"Everett, I've never feared a person so much in my life."

"Don't worry, Lemon. I'm going to talk to her for you."

Soon enough, the room empties. Thirteen walks us out, slinking alongside of us as he lands on the porch, glowing like a dark star.

"Goodnight, Lottie. It's always a pleasure."

"The pleasure is all mine, Thirteen. I'm glad the powers that be are letting you stick around. Get some good haunting in tonight." I give him a little wave as Everett leads me to his car.

"Lemon"—Everett pulls me in close under a full moon surrounded by storm clouds—"I have something to tell you." He sighs hard.

"Oh no. Judging by that expression on your face, it's not good. Oh my goodness, it's Noah. He's died, hasn't he?" Every cell in my body ignites with searing pain.

"No, no, he's fine. He's exactly as we left him. And yes, I'll talk to Suze. I don't want her to do that. But as far as you holding power of attorney—" He bites down on his lip a moment. "Lottie, remember me telling you last month that I'd do everything in my power to hasten your annulment? Well, it's happened sooner than expected. As of two days ago, you and Noah aren't legally married."

"Dear Lord." A brand new level of fright pulses through me. I'm not Noah's wife anymore. I'm right back to being just a baker. And then an idea comes to mind. "Everett, I know exactly how we might be able to wake up Noah. But we have to leave now. Every minute counts."

Just a little over an hour later, Everett and I head up to the second floor where Noah lies all alone in a darkened room. My sleeping prince. He looks so peaceful and at rest, despite the machines they have caustically whirling away. I'm almost afraid to rouse him. But it's for his own good or else his mother will traipse in here and start disconnecting him like an annoying car alarm.

Everett nods as he hands me the platter he carried up for me.

"You're on, Lemon. Do you want me to leave the room?"

"No, please stay. I don't mind at all." I take a step in close to the man who was my precious husband for such a brief moment in time. "Noah? It's me, Lottie. Everett is here with me. We just wanted to come by to wish you a happy Thanksgiving. And, we were sort of hoping you would wake up for us and say those words right back." I look to Everett and take a deep breath. "Here goes nothing," I whisper as I pull the foil off the platter of fresh baked chocolate chip cookies and wave it under his chin. The warm scent of vanilla, brown sugar, and chocolate delights our senses and I'm hoping his, too.

Noah's finger twitches and Everett points to it.

"Did you see that?"

A laugh bubbles from me. "I sure did." I wave the cookies once again and a hard groan moans from Noah.

Everett lands a warm hand over my shoulder. "He's coming back."

Slowly, ever so slowly, Noah rouses to life, his lids fluttering, his mouth struggling as if to say something.

Everett takes off to get a nurse, and just as he leaves the room, Noah's eyes open groggily.

A nurse crashes through the door and quickly checks him before pulling the breathing tubes out of him. Soon, the room is filled with an entire army of nurses, checking his vitals, removing all of those measures that Suze herself wanted gone.

Noah groans once again as he struggles to sit up and they help pull his bed up a few notches.

"Lottie?" My name comes from him hoarse as he looks my way. "I love you."

"Oh my goodness, Noah!" I burst into tears as I hold him tight.

The doctor comes over and smiles down at him. A petite woman who has been a saint to deal with. "You're going to be fine. It's not unusual for this to happen, but I must admit, this is the first cookie miracle I've seen." She chuckles as she looks my way. "He'll still need care and therapy, but if all goes well, he'll be home soon. With an injury like this, you want to be sure to treat the patient with extra care. His body and his mind will be susceptible for a setback in the coming weeks." She looks to Noah. "No hard and fast movements, no rock climbing." She looks my way.

"Nothing emotionally traumatic. Something like that could easily cause a setback, considering the brain swelling he had."

"I won't allow it." I hold up a hand as if taking an oath.

A little over an hour later, Noah is able to sit up on his own. He looks exhausted. A few abrasions from the accident remain under his left eye. The nurses gave him fresh water to drink under their careful supervision, and he's already been given clearance to have one of my magical cookies.

Noah takes a bite and moans. "I've missed this. I missed it and I didn't even know I was missing it."

A warm laugh bounces through me.

Noah looks to Everett. "Thank you for taking care of her. I can never repay you for that." He scowls at him a moment. "Feel free to sleep at your place tonight."

The three of us share a dark laugh.

Noah pulls my hand to him and kisses the ring on my finger. "I'm glad you're still wearing your ring, Lottie. You should. I picked it out and bought it with love. You're my wife." His gaze drops to my stomach. "And that's our baby." His deep emerald eyes meet with mine once again. "We're a family. My wife, my child." His eyes grow glassy with emotion as I look to Everett.

No emotional trauma. Those were the exact words the doctor used. I'll tell Noah the truth about the baby, about us eventually—just not now. There's no way I can risk him falling back into that state.

Not on my watch.

I want to keep him safe, and I'll tell a thousand lies to do it.

And as it stands now, I'll have to do just that.

*Thank you for reading.

Look for **Yule Log Eulogy (Murder in the Mix 16)** coming up next!

Recipe

Pumpkin Pie

From the Cutie Pie Bakery and Cakery

It's Thanksgiving in Honey Hollow and the pumpkin pies are flying off the bakery shelves faster than I can bake them! Even though fall is inundated with delicious desserts of every variety, pumpkin pie, with a large dollop of whipped cream, will always reign supreme for me. This recipe was handed down to me by my sweet Grandma Nell. I hope your family will enjoy it just as much as mine does.

Ingredients Pumpkin Pie

1 can pumpkin puree (15 ounce)

1 can sweetened condensed milk (14 ounce)

2 eggs (large)

1 teaspoon ground cinnamon

½ teaspoon ground ginger

½ teaspoon ground nutmeg

½ teaspoon salt

Ingredients Pie Crust

(Note: Makes two 9 inch pie crusts. You can cover half in plastic wrap and freeze it or double

the recipe for the pumpkin pie filling up above and make two pies!)

2 ½ cups all-purpose flour

1 cup butter (unsalted, cubed, and chilled!)

1 teaspoon sugar

1 teaspoon salt

½ cup ice water

Directions Pie Crust

Preheat oven at 425° F

With a food processor pulse together flour, butter, salt, and sugar. (If you don't have a food processor you can use a large bowl to combine the flour, salt, and sugar. Then add the butter, and combine with a pastry cutter.) Add about a tablespoon of ice water to the mixture while stirring until dough begins to form. You don't need to add all of the water but it's important the butter remain cold during the process so the fats don't melt into the dough. Keeping it cold will ensure a delicious flaky crust.

Roll dough out into a 12 inch circle. Gently lay the rolled out dough into a 9 inch round glass baking dish, pressing the edges gently and crimping as you go along.

You will need to blind bake this crust otherwise it will be soggy if you try to pour the pumpkin pie mixture into it. To blind bake you'll want to set a weight over the bottom of the crust to keep it from puffing up. Use baking beads or plain old beans set on parchment paper to create a weight over the bottom of it.

Bake for 12-15 minutes until crust is slightly golden on the edges.

Directions Pumpkin Pie

Preheat oven at 425° F

In a large bowl whisk together pumpkin puree, sweetened condensed milk, eggs, cinnamon, ginger, nutmeg and salt. Stir until all ingredients are well incorporated. Pour into a blind baked pie crust (see pie crust recipe).

Bake for 15 minutes.

Reduce temperature to 350° F

Bake for 30 – 40 minutes until a toothpick inserted into the center comes out clean.

Enjoy!

Acknowledgements

Thank YOU so much for spending time in Honey Hollow! I hope you enjoyed the adventure with Lottie and all of her Honey Hollow peeps as much as I did. The MURDER IN THE MIX mysteries are so very special to me, and I hope they are to you as well. If you'd like to be in the know on upcoming releases, please be sure to follow me at Bookbub and Amazon. Simply click the links on the next page. I am SUPER excited to share the next book with you! So much happens and so much changes. Thank you from the bottom of my heart for taking this wild roller coaster ride with me. I really do love you!

A super big thank you to Kaila Eileen Turingan-Ramos and Jodie Tarleton. You girls rock and you know it!

A humble thank you to my fabulous betas, Lisa Markson, and Ashley Marie Daniels. Thank you very much for lending me your eyes.

An honorable mention to the fabulous Lou Harper for designing the world's best covers. I can never thank you enough for making the books so magical.

And a gracious thank you to the wonderful Paige Maroney Smith for everything you do. You are the best of the best. There are none like you!

And last, but never least, thank you to Him who sits on the throne. Worthy is the Lamb! Glory and honor and power are yours. I owe you everything, Jesus.

About the Author

Addison Moore is a ***New York Times***, ***USA Today***, and ***Wall Street Journal*** bestselling author who writes mystery, psychological thrillers and romance. Her work has been featured in ***Cosmopolitan*** Magazine. Previously she worked as a therapist on a locked psychiatric unit for nearly a decade. She resides on the West Coast with her husband, four wonderful children, and two dogs where she eats too much chocolate and stays up way too late. When she's not writing, she's reading. Addison's Celestra Series has been optioned for film by **20th Century Fox.**

Made in the USA
Columbia, SC
27 December 2024

50727330R00155